"*Who Killed the Fonz?* stands tall in a field of television property revivals. James Boice deftly mixes the broad comedy of the TV series with classic noir elements, resulting in an unexpectedly emotional roller coaster ride that's more than a novelty. *Happy Days* are here again!"

— Andrew Shaffer, author of the *New York Times* bestseller *Hope Never Dies: An Obama Biden Mystery*

"I must confess that I never watched a single episode of *Happy Days* during its ten-year run, but reading *Who Killed The Fonz?* made me wish I had. Thank you, James Boice, not only for giving us a fast-paced, entertaining novel, but for reminding us in these corrupt Orwellian/Tower of Babel times we live in now that not so many years ago 'friending' someone meant much more than just clicking on a mouse, and that doing the right thing, no matter the risk, was looked upon as honorable and something to be proud of rather than as a sucker's game."

— Donald Ray Pollock, author of *The Devil All the Time* and *The Heavenly Table*

"James Boice has achieved a magic kind of alchemy, exhuming beloved characters from our collective consciousness and gifting them with a fate, a future, and poignant inner lives. *Who Killed the Fonz?* is the best kind of pop-culture hypothetical—one that imagines, with heart, wit, and smarts, what happens when the *Happy Days* fade and real life begins."

— Adam Sternbergh, Edgar Award–nominated author of *The Blinds*

"A wildly inventive and entertaining novel."

—*Booklist*

"Shamelessly entertaining . . ."

—*Kirkus Reviews*

"Readers yearning for simpler times will enjoy this trip down memory lane, which is as comforting as an episode of *Happy Days*."

—*Publishers Weekly*

WHO KILLED THE FONZ?

A NOVEL

JAMES BOICE

*Based on the Happy Days television series
created by Garry Marshall*

SIMON & SCHUSTER PAPERBACKS

New York   London   Toronto   Sydney   New Delhi

Simon & Schuster Paperbacks
An Imprint of Simon & Schuster, Inc.
1230 Avenue of the Americas
New York, NY 10020

First Simon & Schuster trade paperback edition February 2020

SIMON & SCHUSTER PAPERBACKS and colophon are
registered trademarks of Simon & Schuster, Inc.

For information about special discounts for bulk purchases,
please contact Simon & Schuster Special Sales
at 1-866-506-1949 or business@simonandschuster.com.

The Simon & Schuster Speakers Bureau can bring authors to your live event.
For more information or to book an event, contact the
Simon & Schuster Speakers Bureau at 1-866-248-3049 or
visit our website at www.simonspeakers.com.

Interior design by Ruth Lee-Mui

Manufactured in the United States of America

1   3   5   7   9   10   8   6   4   2

Library of Congress Cataloging-in-Publication Data is available.

ISBN 978-1-5011-9688-1
ISBN 978-1-5011-9689-8 (pbk)
ISBN 978-1-5011-9690-4 (ebook)

CONTENTS

SUNDAY

NOTHING WAS MOVING ON THE 405. RICHARD SAT AT the wheel, scanning the Corvette's radio dial, looking for some kind of news about the jam, but there was nothing. He looked at the clock again. Couldn't be late. On the radio was Prince. It was his daughter's favorite. He himself wasn't sure about all that innuendo and raunch. He wasn't sure about much these days. He had seen the film that Prince had starred in and had liked it more than he thought he would. He had expected a two-hour music video, but it was a drama about family and love and what it meant to pursue your dreams—what it cost. His friend Steven had made him watch it. Called him over to his private theater in his house. It had been nice of Steven to call. It had been months. Maybe longer. At one point he asked Richard what he had been working on. All he had to do was tell him about his project. Steven would have helped him. All he had to do was say the words. But Richard couldn't tell him. He muttered that he was tinkering with a few different things, then changed the subject to the new project Steven was executive producing, a time-travel film with the kid from *Family Ties*.

He and Steven had started out around the same time. They were part of a crew of hustlers, strivers, doing whatever they could to make films—Spielberg, Scorsese, Lucas, Cunningham. Back then they all thought it would be Richard who would be the one inviting them over to his private movie theater one day. He had been the first to sell a script, first to get an Oscar nomination. Now almost all of them had become directors on a first-name basis with the world, and he was just another no-name chump stuck in traffic on the 405, running late to lunch with his agent, who held the fate of his project in his hands.

HE STEERED THE CORVETTE DOWN SUNSET. THE CLOCK SAID HE was okay on time. He relaxed, his mind wandering. He wondered yet again whether or not his agent wanting to meet on a Sunday meant good news. Lori Beth and his mother warned him not to get his hopes up. He could not help it. If the news was bad, legendary Hollywood agent Gleb Cooper would not waste his time with a face-to-face. Especially not on a Sunday. Richard had a good feeling. This would be the day he had been waiting three years for.

He passed Book Soup, where it had all started.

He had been browsing the bargain bins when he came across a remaindered copy of a bizarre-looking novel. Black dust jacket, no art—just the title and author's name in big, elaborate font that seemed taken off the side of a nineteenth-century circus wagon. It was the black-and-white author photo that most intrigued Richard. Most of them posed very self-seriously, bloodless Ivy Leaguers in tweed. This one, however, named Cormac McCarthy, wore jeans, denim jacket, had uncombed hair. The look on his face was surprised, like someone had shouted his name and snapped his photo when he turned around. He looked like he couldn't figure out what he was doing on the back of a book jacket. In the background there was not a prestigious college campus or the slick Manhattan skyline but an industrial town. Smokestacks, a bridge, a shipping channel. It looked like the same kind of town Richard had come from.

He took the book to the register. The clerk gave him an approving nod. A good sign. That night at home he started reading.

He could not stop. Three days later, he was still reading. He would have finished the book sooner but the language was like nothing he had ever seen outside of Shakespeare. It was almost something physical to grapple with. He kept having to put the book down and reach for the dictionary. *Concatenate. Leptosome.*

Electuary. They were not even words—they were portals to new worlds.

The story's grip on Richard was just as mysterious. A man lived on a houseboat in Knoxville, Tennessee, in the 1950s. He seemed to have come from a prestigious family but had been somehow alienated or cast out. A sordid cast of fringe-dwelling characters wandered in and out of his life, pulling him into their small-time hustles and drunken misadventures. Not much happened, on the outside. But on the inside, in the heart and mind of this man, named Suttree, as he tried to hold on to his sense of self in an ever-changing world bent on taking it from him, everything was happening. Everything. Richard understood right away that he knew this character. Felt like he had known him all his life. He could not say why. Not since he was a teenager had he felt this way about a book. Something about this novel brought him back to that vulnerable, openhearted place he had been when he was young. And he wanted desperately to hold on to it. Richard did not know why this character was so appealing to him. Because with Richard's sports car and slick suits and Spanish Colonial in Sherman Oaks with a pool and detached mother-in-law bungalow in back, he and Suttree would not seem to have a lot in common. He certainly wasn't a drinker like Suttree. In fact, he rarely drank. Not since one night long ago when he was a young father and the pressure got to him—he took it too far that night and never made that mistake again. But that was what made the book so powerful. It was a kind of art he had never encountered before: the kind that would seem to have nothing to do with you yet still gets to you in ways art that has everything to do with you does not.

When he closed *Suttree* after the final page, he saw the whole thing in his head, the film adaption he would make of this novel. He saw it from the opening theme through the end credits. *I am going to make it*, he told himself. He looked at the cover, then the author photo. He felt a warmth growing in his chest. His fingers and hands filling with blood, like they had been asleep but were now waking up. *I am.* He had to make this film. He was going to write it, and he was going to direct it. It would be his directorial debut.

Not only that—it would be his triumphant return from the brink of extinction.

IT WAS A STRANGE CHOICE OF RESTAURANT. TYPICALLY HIS meetings with Gleb Cooper took place at Musso & Frank, where Gleb had a booth they'd clear out for him upon his arrival, and the maître d' would accommodate his every need. Once Gleb had ordered catfish. The menu did not include catfish. But Gleb wanted catfish, and Gleb got catfish. Richard could not imagine how they located and prepared one so quickly, but it arrived on time with Richard's steak tartare. Richard would try to discreetly eyeball the luminaries filling the surrounding tables without Gleb noticing, because if he caught his companion's gaze wandering like that, he took it as an insult, a challenge, and he would not let it go. He would hold on to it for the rest of the meal. And he would mention it at every meal after. But Richard would tell his grandchildren about that day at Musso's when Warren Beatty came over to their table to shake Richard's hand because, Warren Beatty said, he had just heard from a friend at the Academy that *Welcome to Henderson County* was going to be nominated for an Oscar, and he wanted to shake the hand of the man who had written it.

But this place. It was no Musso's. It was a forgettable Italian spot on Wilshire called Michelangelo's. Richard had never heard of it. There wasn't even a valet. Inside there was no Warren Beatty, nor anybody else, aside from some waiters, a bartender leaning over the want ads of the Sunday *Los Angeles Times*, and Gleb Cooper in a booth.

He almost did not recognize him, because it was the first time he had ever seen him not wearing a suit. He almost did not even see him at all. He had chosen a booth in the corner, in the shadows. He had his head down, reading the paper, a golf hat pulled low. How old was Gleb? Richard could only guess. He had been a ubiquitous presence in Hollywood longer than anyone could remember. But he still maintained the vitality and power of a man Richard's age. He always wore custom suits. He was the one who first encouraged Richard to put more effort and consideration into what he wore. "Dressing well is a way of showing respect," he'd say, "not just for yourself but for everyone else. Give respect, get respect. That's how it all works. That's all you need to know." When Richard first came to town twenty years earlier, he wore the one blazer he had, which was ill fitting and badly cut. He had gotten it off the clearance rack at Gimbels back home, and he wore it until the buttons fell off and his elbows just about poked through. He thought he looked sharp, but looking back on it he probably looked like an overgrown prep schooler. When it wasn't that blazer, it was pastel cardigans—Kmart or Gimbels, whichever was cheaper. Gleb told him he looked like Mr. Rogers. Richard thought it was a compliment, because Mr. Rogers was a good person with a solid character, but it was not. Gleb brought him to the store on Rodeo where he bought his suits, put down a stack of money, and instructed the serious quiet man to take care of his boy. He did. Richard still bought his suits there. Every few years he had them altered to match the changing fashions. Today he was wearing the pale gray double-breasted Calvin Klein. It was Lori Beth's favorite.

Gleb was dressed for the golf course. Richard could not tell if he was on his way to the links or on his way back from them. It seemed to be an important difference. For the first time, Gleb looked to Richard like an old man, shriveled and small, bent as he was with the paper up close to his face, squinting to read it. Richard grew nervous. But then Gleb looked up and noticed him and his voice came booming across the room with the same energy and enthusiasm as always.

"There he is!" Gleb shouted across the empty restaurant. "There he *is*! Get over here! Sit, sit!"

Richard went over and slid into the booth. Gleb was drinking coffee. The waiter poured Richard a cup.

"Thanks for meeting me on a Sunday," Gleb said. "I couldn't wait to talk to you. I was too excited. Are you coming from church or something? What's with the suit? You're making me feel like a schlub."

"Now you know how the rest of us usually feel," Richard said.

Gleb grinned. He smoothed his yellow polo shirt, glancing down at it. "On my way to play some golf."

"No kidding."

"Sunday's golf day. No one is allowed to bother me on golf day. I've turned down meetings with *God* on Sunday. No meetings on golf day. That's my rule. You need rules for yourself. Remember that. Write that down."

A good sign. A great sign. Richard's heart was beating hard. It had to be good news. He fought to control the grin on his face. It was a struggle he had been up against since he had arrived in town. His midwestern grin was its own animal—if he did not take care, the thing would eat his entire head. And in this town, a goofy grin like his was a sign of weakness. If you were going to smile, it had to be cool and confident, like Jack Nicholson's, not unabashed and eager like Richard's.

Stay cool, Richard told himself. *You can celebrate when you get home.*

"I'm flattered," Richard said.

Gleb shrugged. "I'm excited to talk to you. I couldn't wait."

"I'm excited too, Gleb. I can't tell you how happy I am that you see what I see in this project. I know I've sort of been on the sidelines the last few years, but—"

"Sort of? Richard, you wouldn't be more on the sidelines if you were Broadway Joe Namath wearing a Los Angeles Rams jersey in 1977." Gleb laughed at his own joke.

"Got me," Richard said, holding his hands up. "Guilty as charged. It's just that I've wanted to get this project right, you know? I've wanted to take my time with it, make it perfect, and it's been very difficult, it's very dense material, very personal and rich, and, boy, the stream of consciousness of the prose will be very challenging to portray on-screen, but I'm up for it, I really am, I know exactly how to do it." He started to go into the technical approach he intended to take but cut himself short, seeing Gleb's eyes glaze over. "Anyway, I want to thank you for sticking with me and believing in me like you have. I cannot wait to get started."

Gleb said, "Now hold on, Richard, let's back up. What the hell are you talking about?"

"*Suttree*," Richard said, panic creeping in quietly. "We're here to talk about *Suttree*, right?"

Gleb let out a deep, wheezing sigh. "Okay," he said. He waved the waiter over. "Two gin martinis," he said. "Bone dry and dirty." The waiter nodded and left.

Richard understood now, all too well. This is why Gleb

wanted to meet at such an empty, out-of-the-way restaurant. It wasn't that he was embarrassed to bring washed-up talent around to his usual haunt. Though that was clearly part of it. No, it was also out of mercy. Gleb had called this meeting planning to kill Richard's dream but had wanted to spare him the additional pain and suffering of doing it in front of his professional peers, such as they were. He was planning cold-blooded murder en route to a late tee time and didn't want any witnesses.

"Of course a hit job like this would take place in an Italian restaurant," Richard said. Gleb did not seem to hear.

"Look, here it is. Okay? I've met with everyone about your project. *Everyone*. From Warner Brothers to a *guy* named Warner who finances low-budget monster movies for the tax write-off. There is no interest. Zero. I encourage you strongly to forget *Suttree*. Move on. This should help you do that: I got something for you. That's why I wanted to meet today. I have a job for you, Richard."

"If it's writing a *Sorority Slaughterhouse* sequel, forget it."

Richard had written the schlocky slasher film years ago, when he was first starting out. It was the first job Gleb got him. Everyone was doing the same thing, all his friends. Whatever it took. But unlike their films, which were quickly forgotten except among film scholars as their creators ascended to greater things, *Sorority Slaughterhouse* had become a cult hit. For a time it had been a favorite of midnight screenings. Theater owners used to beg for a sequel. Gleb had pressed Richard on it a few times, but Richard had always refused—especially after the Oscar nomination.

"That was a very profitable picture," Gleb was saying, pointing his finger at him. "Don't turn your nose up at it. Be proud of it. You were hungry. You were driven. You were willing to do whatever you had to do. You had grit."

"What do you mean *had*? I still do."

"Sure, sure, yeah, you still do." Richard could tell Gleb was saying it but he wasn't meaning it. "But anyway, Richard, no, it's not that, it's not *Sorority Slaughterhouse.*" He moved his eyes to a point just behind Richard's left shoulder. His face took on an expression of amazement. He raised his hands in the shape of a camera frame, like a cinematographer gauging a shot. Gleb held it there for so long that Richard turned his head to see if something really was back there. Then Gleb announced majestically, jolting his hands at both words for emphasis: "*Space Battles.*" He moved his hands a little lower then jolted them again as he said, "Original Screenplay by Richard Cunningham."

Richard sat forward, his grin coming to life again. He *knew* George, they used to shoot pool together—why hadn't George called to break the news himself? He didn't know he was planning another *Star Wars*. And he certainly had no idea he was thinking of Richard to write it.

"Gleb, that's incredible news. Incredible! *Star Wars! Wow!* I have ideas already. I thought the last installment lacked the gravitas of the original. Man, I'd love to restore some of the seriousness and literary value to the franchise." He let out a whoop that turned the heads of the staff. "Wow, Gleb. I could kiss you. This is exactly what I needed. It's going to change everything for me."

"What? No, Richard, no, not *Star Wars*. *Space Battles*."

"I don't understand."

"A wicked kingdom, an underdog hero, a foxy princess—and all of it in *space*."

"That sounds an awful lot like *Star Wars,* Gleb."

"No. *Space Battles* has two things *Star Wars* does not."

"What's that?"

"Blood and bazoongas." Richard put his hand over his face. Gleb continued. "Did *Star Wars* have blood and bazoongas? No it did not. Think about how much more money it would have made if it had. It's more realistic. It's realism. That's your trip, right, Richard?"

The waiter set down the martinis and a small dish of olives. Gleb speared one and put it between his molars and bit. He lifted one of the martinis and drank. "Drink up," he said, gesturing to the other martini. "Relax. Celebrate. We're celebrating."

"No thank you," Richard said. He and Gleb had worked together fifteen years, and Richard had never been a drinker. Now he was starting to wonder how well his agent knew him. He wondered if Gleb had even read his *Suttree* script.

Gleb reached over and slid the drink like a chess piece to his own side of the table.

"I don't want to do this. I want to make *Suttree*," Richard told him.

"I know you do. But, look, Richard, the days of a movie like that getting made are over. Ten years ago, yeah, maybe. But now? People just don't want it. They want people running for their lives and heroes saving the day. They want the Stay Puft Marshmallow Man exploding over Manhattan. They want Arnold Schwarzenegger and Sylvester Stallone mowing people down. The rest of your generation figured this out long ago. Look at your buddies. Look at Spielberg. Why can't you be more like him? Why can't you just give the people what they want? Now, this job, this is your chance to do that. The kid producing *Space Battles,* his daddy's a shah or a sultan or something, I don't know what he is, but the kid's a *prince.* A real live *prince.* He's got jets. He's got jewels. He's got it all. And he wants to get into *pictures,* Richard. I know this sounds awful to a writer of your caliber, but know what it sounds like to me? *Work.* A *job.* Something you're sorely in need of."

Gleb was not wrong. Three years Richard had spent on *Suttree.* His bank account was low. He and Pepperdine University were square through the rest of 1984, but next year he was not sure where Caroline's tuition money would come from. And there were still the mortgage payments. The city had just bumped up their property taxes. Downsizing was not an option. Not with Marion.

"How much does it pay?" Richard said, looking down at the table, at his hands gripping his thighs.

"Two hundred," Gleb said. "Plus five percent on first-dollar gross."

Richard took a deep breath. "That's good money."

"It's very good money."

It made Richard think.

"What if I wanted to make my movie myself? How much would it cost?"

Gleb laughed and raised his glass to his lips.

"No, I'm serious. How much?"

"Come on, Richard. What you want to do, you'd have to do it on location. You'd have to fly all the actors and crew out to Tennessee or somewhere that can pass for it. That's expensive."

"So you did read my script."

"Of course I did. And I'll be honest. I didn't get it. Neither did anyone else. Also you'd need to hire a director of photography who can figure out how to shoot on a rocking, swaying boat. You'd need to hire a *director*."

"No, that's me, I'll be the director."

"No, no investor would go for it. You don't have the experience. All told, you'd need five million. At least. You're talking about a major uphill climb. Major. I just don't have the time to help you with that. Richard, I'm sorry, but that project is finished. Listen to me: I know what I'm talking about. Take this job. Take *Space Battles*. Knock it out in a few weeks, cash your check, and we'll figure out the next thing. You really have an interest in directing? I'll talk to the prince, see if I can get you a PA position or something. Start getting some experience on set."

Richard glanced around the restaurant. "Funny," he said, "it's not at all like I imagined."

"What's not?"

"Rock bottom."

Gleb sighed and said, "It's not rock bottom. It's *life*. Right now this garbage is all I can get for you. This is it. This is where you are. It's *Space Battles* or nothing."

"Can I think about it?"

"Of course. Take a few days. But I need an answer by Saturday. The prince is leaving the country in two weeks, and we need to set up meetings before he goes. And, Richard, when I say it's *Space Battles* or nothing, I mean it. If your answer is no, I'm sorry, but there's nothing more I can do for you. If you want to continue in this business, you'll have to do it without me."

AS HE DROVE HOME HE KEPT THINKING ABOUT WHAT GLEB HAD said about his friends, the filmmakers he had come up with, many of whom were not only successful writers and not only A-list directors but also serious, big-time producers as well. What Gleb had said was true. The successful ones were the ones who had accommodated the sensibilities of the mainstream. They had not been rigid about their aesthetics. They had found a way to do what they wanted to do while appealing to the masses. They had leveraged their commercial work to facilitate their personal work. Maybe that was the way. One for them, then one for you. What was it that kept Richard from just *doing* that? Why couldn't he just play the game?

That's what it was to people in the industry now, to people like Gleb—a game. A zero-sum one. They read *Variety* for the latest box office figures the way stockbrokers picked apart the Nasdaq reports, the way gamblers chewed up the sports pages looking for any edge. Box office, box scores—they were the same thing to these people. It was not about stories, or film. It was about winners and losers. Nothing in between. He wasn't naïve. Movies cost money. A lot of money. Production, distribution, marketing. None of it was cheap. And the people who put up the money weren't doing it out of benevolence. They expected their investment back and then some. He understood all that. But when it came down to it, he still saw cinema as art, not business. If his goal was making money and working with people only interested in the same, he would have become an investment banker.

And then he would have become a patient in a psych ward.

His more successful friends were drawn to the material they did. They weren't faking it. They had to do their movies the way he had to do *Suttree*. The question was why did he have to do *Suttree*? It was a question he could not answer. The enigma of the creative process, he supposed. Even if he could answer it, he would not want to.

But maybe he *was* naïve. Maybe the reality of making movies was that you had to do what you did not want to do, and he just needed to accept it. Maybe he was still too much of that earnest midwestern kid he once was. Too sincere. Couldn't lie. Couldn't fake it. Couldn't blow smoke. *Didn't* smoke. Too clean for this smutty town. Being married to his high school sweetheart didn't help with this veneer of edgelessness that made him just about disappear. Still madly in love after almost thirty years. Once he went to the Playboy mansion with his friend Brian De Palma, whose latest directorial effort just last weekend opened at $23 million (but who was counting?). It was not Richard's scene. He'd spent the whole party hiding out alone in Hefner's library, reading his first edition *The Great Gatsby.* Now that was Richard's idea of a good time. With charisma like that, maybe it was no wonder he was overlooked.

Then there was the fact that he still lived with his mother.

It had not been planned. After his father passed, Marion decided to just stay out here. She and Howard had been talking about moving to Los Angeles anyway. The weather was nicer, the pace was more mellow, and it would put them closer to their grandkids. It would be better for Howard's heart.

The cardiologist had told them not to make that trip. There was an appointment coming up. A very important appointment. It would give them a better idea of what was wrong this time. Richard begged his father to listen to the doctor. And he could not get them into the ceremony anyway—they would have to watch on TV from Richard and Lori Beth's house. "But what if you win?" Howard kept saying. Richard told him he wouldn't win, there was no chance, not up against *Butch Cassidy and the Sundance Kid*. But Howard would not listen. "Think it's every day my son gets nominated for an Oscar?" He was going to be there in person, no matter what. Richard never for a moment thought he would win, but he was still disappointed when it was not his name they called. Coming home with Lori Beth that night and having his parents there, seeing how proud they were of him, supporting him the way they always had when he was a kid—he was glad they had come. He was relieved.

They all stayed up late that night, Howard telling Richard his favorite parts of *Welcome to Henderson County*. It had not played in Milwaukee. They'd had to drive two and a half hours in the snow to see it in Chicago. When it ended, they rose from their seats and gave it a standing ovation.

"After the show," said Marion, "your father stood outside the theater door, shaking everyone's hands and thanking them for coming, and telling them the writer was his son. He even started signing autographs."

Howard shrugged. "They *asked* me for them."

Before they all turned in that night, Howard stopped Richard at the foot of the stairs. He took his son's face in his hands. "I owned a hardware store," he said.

Richard was confused. "Yeah, Dad," he said. "I know that."

"A *hardware* store. Nails. *Wood.*" Richard did not say anything.

Howard's eyes were glistening, turning red. Richard just looked back into them. "And my son's an artist. A hardware store and my son's an artist." Richard was an inch taller than his father. Howard pulled his head down and kissed him on top of it. "My son's an *artist*."

They were supposed to fly back in the morning. Howard did not come downstairs. Marion kept calling up to him, "We're going to miss our flight!" Finally she went up. Down in the kitchen, Richard and Lori Beth heard her saying his name. Over and over she said it. Soon she was yelling it. Yelling for them.

They buried Howard in Los Angeles. To keep him near his beloved grandkids. Marion took over the empty in-law suite out back by the pool and gave the house in Milwaukee to Joanie and her husband, Chachi.

"My son's an artist." Richard never forgot it. Maybe those words were why he could not bring himself to play the game, to bend and concede.

Richard was lost in these thoughts. He did not see the red light until it was almost too late. He slammed the brakes to avoid making roadkill out of two young women crossing the street. The redhead slammed her palms onto the Corvette's hood.

"Hey man!" she shouted. But it wasn't a she at all. "Get out of the car!" the man was saying.

"Be cool, Axl," said the other one, also a man, who wore a top hat. He pulled Axl away, and they crossed the street. Richard watched them walk off, stapling flyers to every telephone pole they passed, advertisements for their band. He remembered when he used to have that faith and conviction about what he was doing. That grit. He even used to have that red hair. All of it had faded these years under the Southern California sun.

Enjoy it while it lasts, he said to himself.

Then the light turned green and he headed home, to deliver the bad news to Lori Beth and his mother.

AFTER MORE THAN A DECADE IN LOS ANGELES, MARION Cunningham had developed a passion for crystals, star charts, and yoga. She had stopped cutting and coloring her hair after her friends at the holistic health spa had told her that it was where her life force was stored and that toxins from the chemicals in hair dye could seep into the scalp and blood. They tried to convince her about reincarnation, but she couldn't be sold, though she did believe it was a beautiful concept she wished was true. Mostly she was fanatical about her macrobiotic vegetarian diet—she was not allowed to cook for Richard and Lori Beth because they couldn't stand all that tofu and raw alfalfa—but when her grandkids were home she would cook anything they wanted, even meat. It was fine with Richard that she had become so earthly and nonmaterialistic. In her former life as a Milwaukee homemaker, when her days were spent chopping food and sweeping floors and carrying around children and propping herself up, she had taught herself to live without wanting more.

But walking into the house in Sherman Oaks, he was in no mood to receive a lecture on how Mercury being in retrograde had caused the meeting with Gleb to go badly. She and Lori Beth had both warned him not to get his hopes up. He had told them they were wrong. The fact that they were right made it all worse. When he found them in the high-ceilinged living room, sitting on the facing couches in grim silence, he wanted to be anywhere but where he was.

"You were right," he said. "Okay? *Suttree* is done. I was insane for thinking it would ever happen. Of course no one wants a movie like that. And I really believed they might let me *direct* it? Three years of my life—*gone*."

Saying it out loud made him dizzy.

"Oh, Richard," Lori Beth said, looking at him with pity. It was the last thing he needed.

"Sit down, honey," Marion said. She had been crying. It made him realize that Lori Beth had been too. They knew he would be coming home with bad news, he thought. They knew he was going to be destroyed at that meeting, and they let him go into it anyway, they didn't try to shake him out of his delusion.

He turned away from them. "No," he said. He started walking out of the living room. "I need to take a walk or something."

"Richard," Marion said, "sit down." It had been years since he had heard such assertiveness in her voice. He came back and sat in an armchair.

23

"Look," he said, "I appreciate your sympathy. I really do. But—"

"Joanie called," Marion said.

"From Tahiti?" Richard said. His sister and Chachi were there for their tenth wedding anniversary. "Why? Is everything okay?"

Marion cleared her throat and looked at Lori Beth who said, "She was calling about Fonzie."

It took him a moment. The context was too displaced. It was not the name of a producer or an actor or a director or a studio executive. So it did not seem to be the name of anyone. "Fonzie," he said.

Lori Beth breathed deeply and tried to explain. "Last Thursday night, he was driving across Hoan Bridge and . . ." She could not finish.

"And what?" She just shook her head no. She put her hand over her eyes.

"Richard," Marion said. "He was in an accident."

"What happened?"

"Joanie didn't know all the details. She only knew what Al told Chachi when he called to tell them: he lost control of his motorcycle and crashed into the guardrail. He went flying over the handlebars, over the guardrail, and down into the lake. They've been looking, but they haven't found it."

"What do you mean *it?*"

"The body, Richard," Marion said quietly, sweetly. "His body."

Richard was shaking his head side to side, unable to stop. He moved to the edge of his chair, stood up, then sat back down. Lori Beth reached over and put her hand on his. She looked at him with crying eyes.

"I'm sorry," she was saying.

There was a mirror on the wall. Richard could see himself all too clearly in it. Red eyes. Crow's feet. Steadily receding hairline. Inexplicable wobble of flesh beneath his chin—the beginnings of an old man's neck. Each man has that moment in his life when he looks in a mirror and sees for the first time the uninteresting old man young women see when they look at him—*if* they look at him, which, because he's an old man, they do not. This was that moment for Richard Cunningham. Not the day he moved Richie Jr. into his first apartment, and not the day he dropped Caroline off at college. This day. The day he realized middle age had met him like a two-by-four to the face.

The day he learned his best friend from childhood was dead.

MARION AND LORI BETH LEFT HIM SITTING THERE IN THE LIVING room to give him some time alone. He was still there two hours later when Marion returned to check on him. She stood beside him. "You should eat."

"I'm not hungry."

"I'll make you something. No tofu, I promise."

"No thanks, Mom."

She sat on one of the sofas.

"Remember all the things I did just to make a living?" he said. "Lori Beth's and my first few years out here trying to make it?"

"I remember when you were selling watches over the telephone from one of those seedy call centers in Encino, was it?"

"And that was the best one. And all the apartments Lori Beth and I lived in. All those dumps. Mice. Busted plumbing. The police asking about our neighbors."

"I used to worry about you."

"We were fine. It was never dangerous."

"I wasn't worried about your safety, I was worried about whether you were happy."

"I was. Those were some of the best days of my life. We went through times that were so uncertain and so terrifying and made us ask ourselves every day if we should call it quits and just go back home and get more practical jobs, play it safe. But whenever I thought about quitting, you know what I thought about to keep myself going? I thought of Arthur Fonzarelli. I imagined what he would say if I went back to Milwaukee and told him I had quit. I pictured the look in his eyes. How disappointed he would be in me if I ever told him I had stopped believing in myself. He wouldn't have said anything. He would have just looked at me a certain way. I can almost see it now. I would have done any job and lived in a sewer if it meant never having to let him down. So I kept at it."

"He always believed in you."

Richard was quiet. "But then at some point I *stopped* thinking about him. I can't remember when the last time was, before today. I can't even remember the last time we spoke."

"Joanie's wedding," Marion said. "Ten years ago."

"That was the last time I saw him. But when was the last time I spoke to him? I mean, even just on the phone or something?"

"You're being too hard on yourself. You know how he was. It wasn't like he made it easy to stay in touch. When I first moved out here, I used to write all my friends back home letters. Everyone wrote me back. With him, maybe I got a reply once. Once. He just wasn't a letter writer. And he certainly wasn't the type to pick up the phone to chat. We didn't even hear from him when your father died, remember?"

Richard remembered. So many cards and flowers had come in that they had trouble figuring out where to put it all. Other old friends like Ralph Malph and Potsie sent condolences. But there was nothing from Fonzie.

Marion said, "Joanie never mentions his name. I don't think she and Chachi ever saw him around. You're not the only one who lost touch, Richard. It's not your fault. People drift apart. They move on to new selves. It's what happens." She continued, "Joanie said there's a memorial service tomorrow. Back home."

"I don't know why you still call it that," he said.

"I know. Me neither."

"Are Joanie and Chachi going?"

"They said they weren't sure they'd be able to get a flight. And, anyway, Arthur would not have wanted them to cut their trip short. She did say you could stay at the house if you wanted to go back. I thought you might."

"Of course I do. But what about you? You're not going?"

"I don't know—I want to, but tomorrow is tutoring." His mother and Lori Beth volunteered for a charity helping kids who were growing up in rough circumstances stay on track to graduate high school. Tomorrow was their day to help the kids with homework at the community center. "We'll find replacements. Lori Beth is on the phone with them now."

"No," Richard said, "those kids are relying on you. Fonzie would understand more than anybody. It's okay—saying goodbye is something I can do alone."

MONDAY

MONDAY

R ICHARD TOOK A COMAIR RED-EYE OUT OF BURBANK INTO General Mitchell. Walking from the gate to the rental car counter he had the feeling of standing out, of being the center of unwanted attention. It might have been the grief. He could feel it all over himself, like a stink. But it also might have been something else. The people around him were dressed in the prevailing Wisconsin fashion of flannel shirts, work boots, and camouflage hunting jackets. Passing him in the terminal in the opposite direction, their eyes fell on him, and they stared at him with no expression, taking him in like he was an unfunny joke. It made him conscious of what he was wearing. He had not even thought about the Armani blazer and trousers as he was pulling them from his closet in a hurry on his way out the door. Maybe it was the Bruno Magli loafers they didn't like? But it was not just the clothes he wore, or the way he had his Wayfarers hooked in the neck of his shirt. And it was not just his tan, which was hard to avoid when you lived where he did. It was him—there was something about who he was, who he had become, he thought, that did not sit well with these people.

He had forgotten how much they valued the humble and low-key here. He kept that in mind with his choice of rental car: a Ford Tempo, in riveting brown. Driving Highway 100 to the old house, traffic moved briskly. Nothing like rush hour in LA. He scanned the radio, found the rock-and-roll station—the one he had known as a kid was now country and western—which was playing a brand-new song by Don Henley, former drummer of the Eagles, one of Richard's favorite bands. The guitar licks of "Boys of Summer" were edgy and longing and immediately jimmied open Richard's chest and crawled inside. The tune was about looking around one day and realizing your youth had fled out the back window without even thinking to say goodbye. Richard's throat grew tight.

The Henley song faded and a commercial came on. Richard flipped the station. It was a talk radio show. The host and caller were arguing about the Wisconsin governor's election next week.

"Get ready for another term for Johnson," the host said. "He's got too much money, too much machinery. Even a guy with Sealock's charisma can't beat an incumbent like that."

"What about Sackett-Wilhelm?" the caller said. "They were

ready to pull out of here and move to China. They were *gone,* baby. The moving trucks were pulling up to the door. And what happened? Martin Sealock sat down with the CEO and hammered out a deal. Sealock saved thousands of good Milwaukee jobs. What has Johnson done for us working people in this state besides flap his lips? Look at the polls. Sealock was down fifteen points in August. Now, because of what he did for Sackett-Wilhelm, he's within the margin of error . . ."

It felt like they were pounding wooden nails into his skull with rubber hammers. He turned it off. It was exhausting to think anyone could be so caught up in irrelevant nonsense like local politics while ignoring the only news that mattered: Arthur Fonzarelli lay dead at the bottom of Lake Michigan.

HE STOOD IN THE DRIVEWAY OF 565 NORTH CLINTON DRIVE, taking his suitcase from the trunk. His childhood home looked the same, just with different color shutters, window trim, and garage door. Like his high school, which he had passed on the way, it seemed smaller, more modest than he remembered. The trees lining the street, though, were much bigger—their trunks were massive and their bark weathered and thick, their colorful but steadily fading tops reached across the street to almost mingle with those reaching from the other side. *Not clocks and calendars,* he thought, *but trees are what best show the passing of time.* Richard could almost see his father pulling up the street in his DeSoto after another long day at Cunningham Hardware. He could almost see his mother inside through the kitchen window, waving to him, beef stew or rump roast ready on the table. She had been so young when he had been in high school, he realized now. She had been only, what, forty? That was younger than he was now. His father too. Back then, to a teenager, they seemed so powerful and flawless, exempt from all laws of human nature. Now he could see that they were only making it up as they went along and holding their breath, trying not to panic, doing their best to do what was best. It made his heart hurt with a new degree of love for those sweet people who probably weren't nearly as assured as they had seemed to him at the time, who in fact were most likely flailing around in their own heads about what to do in the situations their kid put them in.

And he could almost see Fonzie in the apartment above the garage. He had lived there for a few years. A competing hardware store had opened across the street from Howard's, and the family needed the extra income to make up for the loss in sales. Howard had charged Fonzie fifty dollars a month rent.

It was days until Halloween. To get to the loose brick on the stoop under which Joanie said he would find the key, Richard had to pick through phony cobwebs that clung to his hair.

He opened the door. He had not slept. Fatigue hit him as he stepped inside and turned on the lights. No one was home, but it felt like there was. The place was packed with ghosts. His mother's hatha guru, who was a student of Bikram Choudhury, said the things you did in life remained, reverberated. Actions had reactions, and it all went on indefinitely. An unending chain of cause and effect. The things we did in life stayed behind us, as energy. He knew it was true, because he was feeling it now—his family's energy, his family's history. His youth.

Joanie had modernized the entire interior of the lower level with lush brown carpeting, dusty light blue wallpaper with a floral border, track lighting, glass-top coffee and end tables. He collapsed onto the oversize sectional in the living room and remembered Fonzie laid out on the old one, recuperating after busting his knee. At everyone's urging, he had tried to break a record by jumping fourteen garbage cans on his motorcycle for a *You Wanted to See It*. It was a rare moment in which Fonzie had allowed himself the glory he deserved, had stepped out of the shadows and onto the stage the world was always trying to drag him out onto. He made the jump, but when he crashed on the landing he took it as a punishment for having given in to temptation, influence. For having been full of himself. Everyone called him the Fearless Fonzarelli after that, but he seemed chastened. Quieter, even more reticent.

Richard also remembered when Howard hosted his old army friend's wedding here. It had scandalized the neighborhood because the bride and groom were black. Then there was the time Richard put up a rock band while they were in town on tour, because girls were mobbing their hotel.

In Hollywood when people asked him why he moved away

from here, he had always answered that he needed to be somewhere exciting, that as a writer he needed to live somewhere *alive*. But as the memories came back and he now gave in to his body's demand to sleep, he realized how foolish he had been—there was more life in a day growing up here than in a decade growing old out there.

NO ONE HAD EVER MISTAKEN HIS SISTER FOR JULIA CHILD. THE refrigerator in the kitchen—newly renovated with linoleum tile and wood laminate cabinets—contained little more than condiments, sour milk, and an uncovered plate containing what Richard could only speculate had at one time been a pepper. He resorted to a Hungry Man dinner he found in the freezer. It did not heat evenly nor did it go down easily, but the brownie was delicious. Then he showered and dressed for the memorial service. He had last worn the black single-breasted Armani suit to the funeral of a costume designer he knew who was buried at the same cemetery as Marilyn Monroe. It had fit in well at Westwood Village Memorial Park, but it might be coming on too strong for Heavenly Slumbers Funeral Home in Milwaukee, Wisconsin. But a search of Chachi's closet turned up only suits whose arms hit at his wrists and pants that hit at his shins. Armani it had to be.

He drove the Tempo to the funeral home. The parking lot was full, so he drove around, searching the nearby side streets for a place by a curb, but there was nothing there either. He had to park in the lot of a Kmart a half mile away and walk. He had not thought to bring an overcoat. He had been too distracted, stunned. He had even forgotten a toothbrush. Joanie had extras. But he was shivering by the time he arrived and stepped inside, joining an already immense crowd.

He could barely move. It was mostly women. It was like an open casting call in Studio City, except at casting calls the women all looked the same. These women seemed to represent every varietal of human personality there was, from biker chicks in leather jackets to corporate types in pantsuits and shoulder pads. They were tall, short. Blond, brunette. Straight hair, permed. There was no type. Each was different from the next. What they had in common was Fonzie.

Richard had known many ladies' men over the years. His industry had plenty. It might as well have been a prerequisite for becoming a male lead. Even no-name actors were successful at the single bars. But none of them began to approach Fonzie's degree of proficiency. Ever since they were sixteen years old, all Fonzie had ever needed to do to get a woman to fall in love with him was snap his fingers, and she would come running. All these women had loved Fonzie—even though they knew he did not love them back and probably never would. He cared for them. It did not matter if they were his girlfriend for three hours or three months. But he did not love them. They knew that. It was part of the deal, with Fonzie. They knew the time would come when he would have to go his own way. And when that time came, they understood. It hurt, but only for a little while. He left their hearts intact, so they could love someone else, someone not like him, not fated like he was to forever be alone. Those Hollywood guys' trade was charisma, but Fonzie's trade was respect. Any two-bit lothario can pick up a woman. Only a real man can let her down with dignity. That all these women had shown up today was a testament to which one Fonzie was.

Richard was relieved there was no casket, no body. It was better that way. It was just like the man to not show up at his own memorial service. And Richard would not have been able to stomach a mortician's idea of a waxy, reconstructed Fonzie. It would have been a lie, it would have blown out all the real memories Richard had of him to become the way he remembered him forever. Instead there was a giant photo, propped on an easel. Fonzie sitting on his motorcycle, glaring into the camera, the sun in his eyes. His leather jacket perfect. His black, greased-up pompadour perfect. That was Fonzie. That was how Richard wanted to remember him. You could not tell a lie to that guy in the picture. He would see through it. He saw through all pretenses, all illusions and cons. Whatever you told that guy, the guy in the picture, it better be the truth.

Richard went up and stood close to the picture. Inches from it. Eye to eye. He could almost smell the gasoline, the engine grease. Fonzie had always smelled like machinery. Transport, speed. It was odd looking at a still close-up picture of a man who had so wanted to remain a distant blur to the world. Richard could hear the bike's engine, how it used to rattle the ribs, shake the liver and pancreas into a stew. He could hear the way Fonzie would come through for you, fix your car, or straighten your head about a girl, or even save your life, and then when you thanked him he would say nothing, just shrug and let out a low purring grunt: "*Ay.*"

"HI, RICHIE. REMEMBER ME?"

A small grayed man looked up at him.

"Al," Richard said. "Of course I do." Al Delvecchio owned the diner that had been Richard's teenage hangout. He put his arms around him. "It's great to see you, Al. Great. How are you? You look fantastic." He was speaking in hushed tones, the grief and sadness in the room barely containing the thrill of seeing Al again.

"You too," Al said. "You look like *Miami Vice.* I wasn't sure you'd come."

"Why not?"

Al shrugged. "Big movie star and all."

"Not even close," said Richard.

"Still modest, huh? That's good." His eyes darted down at Richard's blazer then away. Richard thought he seemed to take half a step away from him. He had the feeling of forcing something unwanted on the man. Whatever Al was thinking, he was not saying it. "Look at you. I just want to give you a milk shake and a cheeseburger or something. Remember those days? Every day at two thirty, the high school would let out and here you'd all come, a bunch of rowdy teenagers taking over my diner. An occupying *army*."

"You were a very patient man," Richard said, wincing at what he and his friends must have put him through—the noise and messes.

"Are you kidding? I loved it. You were good kids. When I bought Arnold's Drive-In, I had no clue I'd ever have as much fun as I did when you kids were around. And the way you took me into your circle. That meant a lot to me. I didn't have a lot of friends. Few if any. My life was all business, work. Seeing how important you and your buddies were to each other, that made me realize that I *needed* friends. It changed me. I was different after you kids. I learned how to be a friend. How to *have* friends and how to *be* a friend. Changed my life. Made me a better man. I bet you had no idea, did you?"

"No," was all Richard could say.

"Your group was always my favorite. The ones after you? Forget it. They did not want much to do with me. Didn't matter, I had friends now." He looked around, taking in the room. He shook his head. "Good ol' Fonzie. Taking over my men's room, turning it into his own personal office. Remember? Writing girls' numbers all over the walls. Those were the best days. Magical days."

"How's Arnold's doing?"

"One of those Bennigan's moved in across the street, but we're doing okay. We're hanging on. I've got my regulars. Like those two over there."

Al pointed to the back of the room. Two rather beefy gentlemen lingered in the shadows. They had been staring at Richard's back without his realizing it. He knew because when he turned to look, they turned away a little too quickly. They shifted their weight, muttering to each other, making a big effort to direct their gaze anywhere but at him. They wore modest suits. They would have looked more comfortable wearing fiberglass insulation. Here came Richard's grin again. He went over.

In the twenty years since he had seen them, his old high school buddies Potsie Weber and Ralph Malph had lost hair on their heads and gained it on their faces. Both had mustaches. Both had added twenty or thirty pounds to their bodies, mostly around the gut, and had slight hunches to their shoulders. Richard held out his hand. Potsie looked at it and did not move. Ralph did not take it either.

Potsie said, "Nice of you to squeeze this into your schedule, *Richard*." Ralph laughed bitterly. The grin seeped back beneath Richard's skin and stayed there.

"Well," Richard said, thrown, "hello, guys, how are you? How have you been?"

"Been fine, *Richard*," said Potsie.

"Yeah," said Ralph. "Fine. *Richard*."

He got it. They had known him as Richie. And when he had stopped being Richie and became Richard, it insulted them. Because it had seemed like he was trying to distance himself from where he had come from and who he knew there. And they were right. When he arrived in Los Angeles, no one would take a meeting with a kid just out of the army with no credits, no film school degree, and no connections, who had nothing but the name of a boy. Gleb Cooper started changing the byline on his submissions to Richard, and it helped, if only a little. And a little was better than nothing. So he became Richard. He knew these two would understand if he could only explain it to them. But he did not have the chance.

Because there was a commotion from the entrance. A smattering of applause rose then fell quickly, like someone knew it was not the right time to cheer but could not help themselves. The crowd parted. A man came through who seemed to both float a head above the crowd and also be a part of these people in a way Richard had once been but now was not. This man wore a suit as nice as Richard's. But where Richard's suit seemed like a barrier to the people, the man's drew them toward him. He went to the picture of Fonzie, lowered his head, stood there with his hands folded and eyes closed, paying his respects.

Potsie turned and said to Ralph, purposefully loud enough for Richard to overhear, "Now there's a guy who never forgot where he came from."

"What's he doing here?" said Ralph. Potsie shrugged.

The man turned away from Fonzie's picture and glanced in their direction. He looked astonished. He came over.

"Excuse me," he said. "You're Richard Cunningham."

"I am," Richard said slowly. He had never been recognized in public.

The man smiled and laughed. It was an imperfect smile that went up much higher on one side of his face than the other. "You wrote my favorite movie." He took Richard's hand in his and shook it. "*Welcome to Henderson County* is a masterpiece."

Richard felt his face burn up. "Thank you," he said.

"Martin Sealock," the man said. "It's an honor to meet you."

Richard knew the name but could not place it.

Potsie said to Sealock, "Sir—"

Sealock said to him, "Martin. Please."

"Oh my name's not Martin, sir, it's Potsie—Potsie Weber. But I just wanted to tell you that you've got our votes. Ours and everyone else at Sackett-Wilhelm. You really came through for us."

"All the way," said Ralph.

Now Richard knew who this was. The candidate for governor, from the radio on the drive from the airport. His natural charm and unforced charisma reminded Richard of John F. Kennedy, whom Richie canvassed for in 1960.

"You knew Fonzie?" Richard said.

"He was my mechanic." Then he added, "Best in the state."

"Best in the *country*, Fonzie would have said." They all smiled.

"Most honest too," Sealock said. "Margo and I didn't trust

anybody else with our cars." He tried to catch the eye of one of the women standing in front of Fonzie's photo. The others were moving past it in a steady stream, but she stood still. They had to part to get around her. She stood out even among all the beauties in the room. She was tall, with a short New Wave haircut, porcelain skin, and bold red lips. She saw Sealock was looking for her and came over. "Know who this is?" Sealock said to her. "Richard Cunningham." She looked at her husband blankly. She turned to Richard, blinking, seeming to search her brain for where that name had been stored away. In her eyes Richard saw what he took to be worry about coming up empty and seeming rude.

Sealock helped her out. "He wrote *Welcome to Henderson County.*"

"Of course," she said. She got her bearings. "Of course. What a pleasure." She took Richard's hand and leaned in, saying to him, "We own it on LaserDisc. I think this one's watched it a thousand times. Which means *I've* watched it a thousand times. Which is fine by me. It's a beautiful film."

Sealock said, "How did you know Fonzie?"

"We grew up together."

"We all did," said Ralph.

An aide was pulling Sealock away. "I'm sorry to have to run," he said. "We have a campaign event at the hospital. Richard, it was a pleasure." They all shook hands. Sealock had not gotten very far before he turned and came back.

"I have an idea," he said. "Richard, how long are you in town?"

"I fly back tomorrow," Richard said.

"Oh. That's too bad."

"Why?"

"The polls say this election is going to be the closest race in state history. We need every advantage we can get. My team is telling me we need one final television ad to run this weekend to, we hope, put us over the top. I wouldn't be able to face all the people working themselves to the bone for this campaign if I knew I missed the chance to have the great Richard Cunningham write it for us. What do you think? Would you consider it?"

It would be the chance he needed to make peace with the place and people that had raised him. It would also be a good distraction to work again.

"Of course," he said.

"Where are you staying? I'll give you a call tonight to talk more."

"I'm staying at my sister's."

"What's the number?"

Richard gave it to him, and the aide took it down.

Martin and Margo Sealock left again. Potsie half turned to Richard. "Making business moves at a memorial service? Real nice."

He felt a sharp pain in his side. "Come on," he said, "that's not what it was."

Potsie said, "Whatever you say."

Ralph said, "Yeah, whatever you say, *Richard*."

• • •

RICHARD STEPPED OUTSIDE. THE COOL, FRESH AIR TASTED GOOD
after the air inside—hot from the crowd, sour from the animosity
of jilted old friends, repressive all around. He would have stayed
longer if not for Potsie and Ralph. What could he do to make
them see he wasn't as coldhearted as they had made him out to
be in their minds over all these years? How could he shatter that
mythical version of him they had created? How could he become
their friend again?

The already capacity crowd for the memorial service had
grown since Richard had arrived. With no more legal spaces re-
maining, the latecomers were forced to park their cars in front
of fire hydrants, in bus lanes—even up on the sidewalk. Richard
stood there for a moment, moved at this testament to Fonzie's
popularity. Sealock was still there, arguing with a police officer.
The cops were there ticketing the illegally parked cars.

"You can't ticket cars at a memorial service, Kirk. It's not right."

"What's not right is parking where you're not allowed. And
it's *Lieutenant* Kirk."

"For now, maybe," Sealock said.

"What's that supposed to mean?" Kirk said.

"Figure it out," said Sealock, turning and walking away to
his waiting Town Car. There was a ticket on the windshield. He
snatched it off, shaking his head in anger.

In the 1960s, Officer Kirk had spent most of his hours as a

patrol officer hounding Richard and his teenage friends over any petty grievance he could dig up—or *make* up if he had to. He was hardest on Fonzie. He was always arresting him or doing his best to harass him out of town—usually for nothing more than liking motorcycles and rock and roll. Richard walked in the other direction, going out of his way to avoid the cop.

He was still within earshot as he crossed the street. "Forget the tickets," he heard Kirk saying to his subordinates, "call in the tow trucks."

Richard took one last look over his shoulder. Kirk was looking right at him. He turned and picked up the pace.

HE DROVE AROUND FOR A WHILE, LOOKING FOR A SUSHI PLACE. He had never even heard of sushi when he was growing up— now he was addicted. The closest he could find was a Long John Silver's. He almost did it too—he went inside and got all the way up to the counter before admitting that he did not have the guts.

Instead he went to Arnold's Drive-In.

The Bennigan's across the street had people standing on the sidewalk out front waiting for tables. Its lot was full. The lot at Arnold's had only a few cars—Hondas, mostly, and Volkswagens. Foreign made. In Richard's day a foreign car was anything made outside Detroit. Back then, this lot would have been filled with American hot rods or the Ford Falcons kids had begged, borrowed, or stolen from their parents.

Richard stepped out of his car and into a day from the past. It was an unremarkable day in 1958 or '59. An afternoon, after school. He was behind the wheel of his father's car. The windows were down. The sun was out. Bobby Darin was singing "Splish Splash" on the radio. A girl was in the passenger seat—Mary Lou Milligan, maybe, or Cindy Shellenberger. Outside across the lot his friends were waiting for him, Potsie itchy to lay out whatever latest new hustle he had in mind. An unremarkable day, one that at the time would have seemed to mean very little. But now he could see those were the best kind. They were everything.

He went inside.

The old soda fountain that had once served milk shakes and root beer floats now also served booze. Bellied up to it were factory guys in blue jumpsuits holding cans of beer. Some wore SEALOCK FOR GOVERNOR hats. The beer was Shotz. What his father used to drink. Fonzie had had two friends who worked at the brewery, Laverne and somebody—Pinky, it might have been.

No matter. He found an empty stool, and the bartender came over.

"What'll it be?"

"Milk shake."

The guys at the bar glanced at him. One of them muttered something he did not hear. It made the others snicker.

Richard took in the room around him. It had been perfectly preserved. The mottled gray floor, the wood paneling on the walls, the green swinging door into the kitchen, the college pennants everywhere. Those aluminum napkin dispensers, those brown pads on the booths. All the little things he had forgotten he remembered.

In one of the booths were Potsie and Ralph. They did not notice him, and he did not go join them. He knew they did not want to talk to him.

He saw the jukebox.

He stood and went over to it. This jukebox and Fonzie had always had a special relationship. He was the only one who could work it. Kids like Richie would pump in the quarters, push the buttons, and get nothing. But one cool knock from Fonzie's elbow and it would whir to life and they'd all dance to "Rock Around the Clock."

Richard tried it now. Banged his elbow against it. Nothing—just pins and needles in his pinky. He put in a quarter and tried again. The factory guys were snickering at him again.

"That thing doesn't play Madonna, buddy." They laughed.

Richard laughed too, like a good sport. He didn't try to explain. He gave up, leaving the jukebox sitting silently, and went back to his barstool.

"This is a local legend you're messing with," said a voice behind him.

It was Ralph. He and Potsie had come over for another round and overheard. It was one thing for them to give their old friend a hard time, but it was another to see others do it.

"Oh yeah?" one of them said.

"Yeah. He's a writer. A famous one, out in Hollywood. He won an Oscar."

"Nominated," said Richard.

"He was nominated for an Oscar," Ralph said. "And he was coming to Arnold's when you knuckleheads were still in diapers."

Potsie gestured to the one on the far end of the bar and said, "Course we all know Jeff here's still in diapers."

The others cackled.

"Only for Packers games," Jeff said. "So I don't have to get up and go to the bathroom. It's smart."

The others started in on Jeff as the bartender gave Richard his milk shake.

Potsie and Ralph got their beers. Richard expected them to go back to their booths, but they stayed there, standing on either side of him.

Richard did not know which direction to go in with them. What to say. Start simple. "You know these guys?"

"We work together."

"Sackett-Wilhelm, right? What do you do there?"

"Me, I operate a crane," Ralph said. "Potsie here sleeps under his desk and eats lunch."

Potsie rose to his own defense. "I oversee quality control."

Then it fell quiet. They did not have much to say to each other. Or maybe they had too much. It was all logjammed somewhere inside them. Nothing could get out.

"We were sorry to hear about your dad," Ralph said.

Richard said, "Thanks. It was a long time ago."

"Doesn't matter how long ago it was."

Richard said, "No. It doesn't."

"He was a great guy."

"He was," Richard said, too quickly, dismissively. Then he said again, more slowly. "Thank you. He was."

Then it fell quiet again. There were so many years between them. In each of those years were hundreds of things they had known deeply and intimately that the other hadn't and never would. Their kids' faces. Their wives' voices. The jobs they went off to. The insides of their own heads. Richard was seeing his own two previous decades scroll past—the various LA apartments where he and Lori Beth had lived. His daughter crying right after she was born. The friends out there, who themselves were old friends now. He didn't know what he had in common with Potsie and Ralph anymore. They had shared so much once. They had sharing everything. Then they had shared nothing. It made Richard feel upside down.

Then—what was he thinking? Of course. They still shared something. The obvious.

"To Fonzie," Richard said.

He raised his milk shake. Ralph and Potsie lifted their beer cans.

"To Fonzie," they said.

The logjam was broken. Potsie laughed. "Hey, remember

when he got my bicycle back from that gang after they stole it from me?"

"Not before we tried to get it back ourselves," Ralph said.

"The Dukes," Richard said.

"I can't believe you remember their name," said Potsie.

He ran a hand over his face, appalled at his own youthful idiocy. "We showed up at their *hangout*."

"That pool hall, over on Seventeenth Street."

"'Give it back!' They would have murdered us."

"But then Fonzie showed up," Richard said. "Out of nowhere. Had a dozen of the toughest guys in town with him. They were only there to play pool or something, but the Dukes thought they were there to fight them. Which is what Fonzie wanted. It worked. The Dukes were scared out of their minds."

Potsie laughed, shoulders shaking, eyes squinted. "They vanished quick, didn't they?"

"Left your bike for you."

"Yes they did. Yes they did."

"Richard," Ralph said, "remember when you were home alone and someone broke into your house?"

"Geez," Richard said, shuddering, as if the horror was fresh, "yes, now I do."

"And somehow you managed to call Fonzie? How'd you call Fonzie?"

Richard said, "The guy made me order a pizza. He was hungry or something, who knows. I dialed Fonzie's number instead.

'Hello, I'd like one large pepperoni pizza please.' At first Fonzie goes, 'Are you out of your mind, Cunningham, what are you doing?' Then he figured out I was in trouble."

Ralph snorted and shook his head in disbelief.

Richard said, "He came over and locked the guy in a closet, and the cops came and got him. And the kicker? *He brought the pizza.*"

They were laughing hard now.

Ralph said, "Remember when he jumped the shark?"

"On the water skis?" Potsie said. "Who could forget? It was out on Lake Michigan. The shark was in a tank, Fonzie was going to jump over it, there was a ramp set up. There was no way Fonzie would make it over. We all thought he would be bait. Remember, Richard?"

Richard said, "Are you kidding? Who do you think was driving the speedboat? *You* might have thought he'd be bait. I never had any doubt he'd make it."

"And he made it," said Ralph. "He jumped it."

"Jumped the hell out of that shark," said Potsie.

Ralph said, "Kept his leather jacket on too."

"Kept it *dry,*" said Richard. "I told Spielberg that story."

"Steven Spielberg?"

"Steven Spielberg." Ralph and Potsie sat up and turned toward Richard, giving him all their attention. "In fact, *Jaws?* The original draft of the screenplay? Had that story in it. There was a scene where a guy on water skis jumps a shark."

Potsie slapped the bar. "No kidding. Why'd they cut it?"

"The robot shark ended up being more expensive than they thought, and they didn't have money to shoot that scene."

Ralph said, "Wait a minute, that's a robot shark?" Potsie and Richard gave each other a look, smirking. "The shark in *Jaws*? That's not a real shark?"

"No," said Richard, "it's real."

Ralph looked relieved. "Okay, good, because I was going to say: if it's a robot shark, the movie completely falls apart. All they'd have to do is take its batteries out."

Potsie turned to Richard. "How's work?"

Richard said, "Work? It's good. Work is good." He thought his voice sounded artificially cheerful. He felt as though they were picking up on it.

"Yeah?" Potsie said. "Got any movies coming out?"

"Sure," he lied, "sure."

"Like what?"

"Well," said Richard, "a few things. They're, you know, in various stages of development."

"Yeah, development," echoed Potsie knowingly, as if fluent in industry jargon.

"What are they?"

"Well, okay, one of them is kind of a sci-fi project." He hoped that would satisfy them, but they stared at him, waiting for more. "There's a wicked kingdom, an underdog hero, a foxy princess— and get this: it's in *space*."

"Wait wait wait," Ralph said. "You're—" He covered his mouth as though there was something vulgar in there he did not want coming out. He lowered his voice. "You're doing a new *Star Wars?*"

Potsie said, "Oh, man, *Star Wars.* That's why he's being so coy about it. They're real secretive about that stuff out there in Hollywood."

Richard could not bear to disappoint them. And maybe he wished too much it was true, that he was the kind of guy who would get such a job.

"You got me."

Ralph turned to the guy at the bar next to him and nudged him. "This guy's writing the next *Star Wars.* He's my buddy. We're buddies."

Richard changed the subject. He asked them about their families. Potsie had two girls, both in high school. Ralph had a fifteen-year-old son.

"I'm teaching him how to play bass," Ralph said.

Potsie said to him, "*You* should learn first."

"You guys still play?" Richard said.

Potsie grinned. "We got the band back together. Remember the band?"

Richard said, "We weren't bad, were we? Played a pretty mean 'Splish Splash.'"

"Still do," said Potsie. "Me and Ralph and a couple of guys from work. We jam in Ralph's basement a couple nights a week.

Drives Jeanette bonkers. All she wants is some peace and quiet to do her Jane Fonda workout tape. Instead she gets us and our racket."

"Come on," said Ralph. "It's not that bad."

"Not that bad? She walks around with tissue stuffed in her ears."

"It's your singing, is what it is."

"Oh please."

"Playing out anywhere?" asked Richard.

"Sure, sure," said Ralph.

"No," said Potsie.

Ralph said, "Not yet, no, but soon, probably. We've got a vision, Richard. This isn't just for fun. This has a real shot. We've got a *sound*. In fact, I just blew a bunch of money on recording equipment. A real high-end microphone and reel-to-reel tape system. We're gonna record a demo tape, bring it around to some record labels. You should hear us, we're good, we're real good, it's a slam dunk that we'll get a record deal. We sound like Springsteen."

Potsie said, "*Better*. We sound *better*. Know why? Because we're the genuine article." Ralph nodded, looking off at nothing, full of himself. Potsie continued, "Springsteen—what does that guy know about the working life? He's never set foot in a mill. We do it every day. So we figure, if he can make millions singing about the working life, why can't we?"

"That's right," said Ralph.

Richard said, "Gosh that was fun, being in that band. We had *fun* back then. I don't have fun like that anymore."

Potsie said, "Still play at all, Richard?"

"Not really. I sold my sax when I got to LA for rent money. Maybe every now and again, I'll take the guitar out of the basement, but, you know, the strings are all rusted and out of tune, and I can never get around to putting new ones on. I'll play long enough to cut my fingers up then put it away." He said, "You have a name?"

"We do," Ralph said proudly.

"Men Who Work," said Potsie. "Originally we wanted Men at Work, but it was already taken."

Richard said to him, "Remember when Fonzie filled in for you, when you couldn't make the gig? Man, he was so nervous about singing in front of all those people. I'd never seen him like that. But once we started up on 'Heartbreak Hotel,' man, he brought the house down. The guy was unbelievable. He could do anything he wanted. The world was his, you know?" Richard continued, "There are so many things I want to ask him. I wish I knew his *life*. What was he *doing* all these years?" Potsie and Ralph did not say anything. "I mean, what had he been *doing*? You know? How did he turn out?" Potsie and Ralph looked at each other. "What?"

Ralph said, "Nothing, it's just—we don't really know. We didn't really know him anymore. We'd see him around town sometimes, but . . ." Ralph shrugged. "We didn't really talk or anything."

"You're telling me you two were living in the same town with him all this time and don't know if he got married or something?"

Ralph said, "Definitely was not married. If we knew one thing about him, he never lost his touch with women."

Potsie said, "My kids used to look for him around town, try to spot him when we were in the car. There he is! The Greaser Guy! They thought he was funny, with the jacket and the sideburns and everything. To them, you're only cool if you're wearing acid-washed jeans, drive a Lamborghini, and have hair like Duran Duran. They didn't know who he was, to them he was just a local character out of step with the times, you know?"

"Did you tell them who he was?"

"Yeah. But they didn't really get it."

"Why not?"

"I don't know, you know how kids are. It was their game, and Dad was intruding. But, you know, I'd try to wave or honk at him. But it was like he never saw. He stopped coming around after you left."

Ralph said, "The only reason he ever let us hang out with him in the first place was because of you."

"That's not true," Richard said. "He loved you guys."

"He *tolerated* us," Ralph said. "He loved *you*. You were the link. As far as we were concerned, when you left, Fonzie might as well have too."

Potsie said, "All I know is he was still a mechanic, and he still had the motorcycle and the leather jacket and the women. The guy's life began at age sixteen and stopped at age twenty-five. Period. No childhood, no adulthood. Eternal young man. That's why he is, was, and ever shall be the coolest."

"Amen," said Ralph.

"I was thinking about that earlier," Richard said. "The women part especially. The crowd today was impressive. But, I don't know, it also made me a little sad for him. Part of me would rather one woman showed up for him—just one—instead of a thousand. One woman who had been there for Fonzie all these years, through all the hard stuff, who knew him better than anyone. I was thinking of Lori Beth. I want Fonzie to have known what that's like, to have a partner committed to riding out every storm, who'll be there for you no matter how bad it gets. I want Fonz to have had that. I hope he did. But after today, it doesn't seem so."

They sat there in silence for a few moments.

Richard said, "What happened to his bike? Is it in the lake too?"

Potsie said, "No. But I heard it's totaled. They probably scrapped it."

"I still don't understand how he crashed."

"I mean, you know, it was rainy. It was foggy."

"But he'd ridden in those conditions a thousand times. And he knew that bridge. He knew what he was doing. He was always careful."

"All it takes is one slipup," said Potsie.

Ralph said, "It's like Kirk told the papers. He skidded out and hit the guardrail. Went flying over. He might have walked away if it hadn't happened where it did, on the bridge."

Richard said, "Kirk." He stuck his finger into his mouth and pretended to puke.

Ralph chuckled. "Remember him from the old days, huh?"

"I could have gone the rest of my life without seeing that nasty little face again. I can't believe he's still around."

"Not only is he around—he's in *charge*. He runs the show over there," Potsie said. "And he hasn't changed a bit. Just has more power now. You can imagine what that's like."

"It's tragic," Richard said. "When we were kids, Fonzie seemed invincible. The one thing you could always count on was that he would show up and save the day. And that no matter what, he would be all right in the end. He was like Superman. And what ends up taking him out? A puddle."

"Look," Potsie said, "he wasn't invincible. He wasn't Superman. He just seemed that way to us because we were kids. Fonzie was a human being. He was a *guy*, a great guy, sure, an incredible guy, but in the end? Just a guy. Whose life was just as fragile as anybody's. He would have been the first to say it: any of us, anytime, one wrong move." He snapped his finger. "In a blink. Even Arthur Fonzarelli."

"No, you're right," Richard said. "You're completely right. He was just a person. And we were just kids."

"Just kids," Potsie said.

"Everyone gets old," said Ralph. "No one stays cool forever. Not even the Fonz."

THE MEN'S ROOM AT ARNOLD'S USED TO BE FONZIE'S OFFICE.
More often than not you could find him here, standing at the mirror combing his hair, reluctantly dispensing his wisdom to an eager gaggle of the uncool—Richie often among them—or adding another girl's phone number to the wall he used instead of a little black book. Once in sophomore year of high school Richie scored with a girl. *Scoring* back then meant making out a little in the back seat up at Inspiration Point. A momentous occasion. A breakthrough after years of struggle. He thought he was a man afterward. Life from that moment felt clear, laid out in a simple, orderly grid: Richie Cunningham, women, constant scoring—manhood. But the girl turned out to be Fonzie's girlfriend. The guy went through them fast—who could keep track? Richie was not a man after all. He was a creep, he was worse than a creep, he was a subspecies of base humanity. And he had committed a terrible crime against the toughest guy in town. Before this, Richie had not known where he stood with Fonzie. It seemed like Fonzie had been giving him a chance, for reasons Richie could not comprehend. The distant, dangerous hood had begun sitting near Richie and his friends at Arnold's, listening

to their conversations. He would even sit with them sometimes, and they'd talk like something approaching friends. In those moments, Richie felt all lit up inside. Like he *existed*. He would look around the room, seeing if others were noticing that Fonzie was sitting with *him*, if others were seeing that he was *visible* now. But other times, Fonzie would act like Richie did not exist. Look right through him in public. Not answer him when he spoke to him. That made more sense to Richie. He felt more comfortable when that happened. The guy associated with bikers, hustlers. He was hard. Never smiled. Always seemed to simmer with anger. Why would Fonzie want to be friends with a Boy Scout like Richie? He could not tell what it was—if Fonzie liked him, or just saw him as something to look at and listen to when there were no better options.

When Fonzie found out what Richie had done, he summoned him here to this very bathroom. To kill him.

There was no escaping the inevitable. Richie went. Potsie and Ralph stood outside the door, praying for him. His knees were shaking. His mouth felt like a bag of peanuts. He was already feeling little flashes of what the pain would feel like all over his head and body.

Fonzie stood there, gripping the sink, his back to Richie. Wouldn't even look at him. Finally, Richie said, "Well, go on. Get it over with."

Fonzie didn't move.

Richie said, "Whatever you're going to do to me, I deserve."
Then he said, "What *are* you going to do to me?"

Fonzie said, "I don't know." Then he said, "I mean, I don't
want to do anything."

Richie did not understand.

Fonzie said, "But I have to. I have to hurt you, Cunningham.
You know that."

Richie did. Reputation was everything to the Fonz. It was his
most secret weapon against a world that wanted nothing but to
push him around. If word ever got out that Fonzie let Richie's
transgression go unpunished, it would open the gates, and rush-
ing in would come every other cheat and manipulator and liar,
every self-serving double-talker, running over each other to try
and take chunks out of him until there was nothing left. That was
the world, as far as Fonzie was concerned. Living meant protecting yourself from it.

He took a step toward Richie. Just that step made Richie
flinch. Fonzie stopped. "Know what I've been doing, when I've
been standing here waiting for you? I've been trying to get myself angry, you know? Angry enough to fight you. But all I keep
thinking about is that mechanical Santa."

The previous Christmas, Richie got a present for Fonzie—a
three-in-one wrench. On Christmas Eve, he dropped in on him
at his garage to leave it for him, thinking he would be with family
somewhere like everyone else. But Fonzie was there, he was sitting

all alone, eating food out of a can. The guy had nowhere to go, no family. Fonzie would not have liked Richie knowing this about him, so he left before Fonzie saw him. He went home and talked to his father about it, and they returned to the garage together and convinced Fonzie to come join them at their house. He had too much pride to accept that kind of pity—they had to lie that they needed his help fixing the broken mechanical Santa Claus for the front yard. He fixed it for them, and they fixed his Christmas. He even said grace at dinner. "Hey God," he prayed, "thanks."

"Nobody was ever nice to me like that before," he said now.

"What are you saying?" Richie said. "That it evens out? Good deed, bad deed?"

"No, what I'm saying is I don't want to hurt my friend."

Richie said, "Friend?" He smiled. "Did you just say I'm your friend?"

Fonzie did not answer. He did not have to.

Then he said, "Anyway, truth is, even if I wanted to wallop you I probably wouldn't do a very good job. I haven't been in a fight in years."

"That's ridiculous. I don't believe it for a second. You're the toughest guy in town. You fight all the time."

"No, see? That's just my reputation. If you represent yourself right, your reputation does all your fighting for you. What's important isn't whether you're tough, but whether or not people *think* you are. It's been years since I've thrown a punch. Now if you tell anybody that, that will no longer be the case."

"Your secret's safe with me."

"I don't want to hurt anybody. Not my friends, not anybody."

"So what do we do?"

It was a conundrum. They talked it over. A serendipitous solution was reached when the door opened while Richie was standing near it and smacked him in the face, giving him a black eye he let everyone attribute to Fonzie.

The girls' phone numbers had been painted over years earlier, replaced by new vandalism—a limerick about Heather Locklear from *Dynasty*, and the apparently controversial statement that Ozzy Osbourne ruled more than Iron Maiden. Being a writer, Richard always had a pen. He took it out of his pocket and wrote right where the man himself would have, once upon a time:

Long Live the Fonz

–RC

WHEN HE RETURNED TO THE HOUSE THE RED LIGHT ON THE answering machine was blinking. He hit PLAY. The tape rewound, then the beep sounded, followed by a voice that was still big despite being staticky and faint over a long-distance wire.

"Richard! Gleb Cooper, how the hell are you? Your *wife* gave me this number, said I could reach you here. She *told* me about your loss, my sincere and heartfelt condolences. I know it's a difficult time and I'm slime for asking, I don't mean to push, but *when you're ready* we need to touch base about *Space Battles*. I just got off the phone with the prince. He's asking for an update. He's *excited*, Richard. *We need to give him an answer by Saturday.* Call me, please. Again, my sincere and heartfelt cond—"

Richard went to the next message.

"Hello, Mr. Cunningham," said a woman's voice. "This is Margo Sealock. It was a pleasure meeting you today, considering the circumstances. Martin and I would love to host you tomorrow morning at our home to discuss the campaign ad we mentioned, if you're available. Will ten o'clock do?" She provided the address and left a number to call to confirm. He called it back, left a message: He'd be there.

He picked up the phone and dialed Lori Beth. He sat in the recliner and tried to tell her everything about the trip, the calling hours, the people he saw again. He tried, but he couldn't get it all across. It was too immense. All he could do was give her basic facts: who, what, where.

"So it's real," she said.

"It's real."

"It's just starting to sink in for me," she said.

"I miss you," he said.

"I miss you too. But you'll be back tomorrow."

"Yeah. No, wait. It looks like I'll need to stay another day or two. Some work has come up." He told her about the Sealock job.

She said, "It's exciting. It's just like Fonzie that something good will come out of this."

After they hung up, Richard called the airline to change his flight then opened a Tab he found in the fridge and turned on Joanie's big-screen Magnavox. *Letterman* was on. They were racing office chairs on skateboards propelled by fire extinguishers. It reminded him of things he, Potsie, Ralph, and Fonzie used to do for fun when they were kids. It went to commercial and an ad for Governor Johnson came on. A serious man wearing a suit an IRS agent might wear was seated at a desk in an office. The shot was poorly framed—the governor was off-center, and you could see the boom mic dropping in and out from the top. The zoom went in, pulled back out, slammed back in again. It was never completely in focus. Johnson spoke in a monotone: *Abatement spending for the industrial sector should forfeit the budget rights of the tax cuts to the economy* . . . Richard zoned out. Nothing but more noise in a world of it. No one needed another guy in a suit on TV lecturing them with wonky gibberish. People craved honesty. They needed it. An honest piece of cinema would get their attention. That's what Richard would do for Sealock.

TUESDAY

RICHIE ONCE HAD A DATE WITH A GIRL WHO LIVED IN Whitefish Bay. When he rang the doorbell to pick her up and take her to Arnold's for dinner, he felt like he was made up not of cells but of insufficiency. Whitefish Bay was the neighborhood where the chief executive officers lived, the chairmen of the board. She was nice, but so is everyone, he thought, and she could see it all in his eyes. He was quiet on the drive. The words just would not come. She asked him what was wrong, but he could not tell her. He gave her nothing. What was the point? He wasn't rich. She would never be interested in him. They did not even make it to Arnold's before he told her this was a mistake, that they had better call it a night. She was confused, she protested that he was wrong. But he turned the car around.

When he dropped her off back at her house and drove away, he was relieved. He felt like he had been smart enough to avoid something. He went on to Arnold's. Fonzie was there. Fonzie said, "What are you doing, where's your date?" Richie told him. "Cunningham," Fonzie said, "you idiot. She liked you. She didn't care that you weren't rich. If she did, she wouldn't have gone out with you in the first place. The only one who had a problem with you was *you*. You could have had a beautiful date with a fantastic girl. But you put things into her head that she didn't have. That's not fair to her. And now you've got nothing. That's what you get for being so smart." Richie knew Fonzie was right. He asked her out again. She said no. She was not interested in someone so insecure. Next time he saw her, she was following Fonzie around, begging him to notice her, to take her out. He never did. It was an important lesson, and one Richie remembered the next time he met a girl he thought was out of his league: a tall brunette in a library named Lori Beth.

Now, after a career spent attending cocktail parties in Beverly Hills and meetings with film industry power players in Bel Air, Whitefish Bay seemed less daunting than it had that night. He wished he could go back and do it over. He would knock on the door, his eyes steely, unfazed. She would smile, like she had the first time, but now he would believe the smile, he would not try to guess what she was thinking behind it. In the car, he would have all the words.

There was not much about youth that was not simply regret.

• • | • •

THOUGH MOSTLY THESE HOUSES NOW WERE NO LONGER THE
castles they had been, Sealock's house was an exception. The massive stone-and-wood French Normandy mansion on a densely treed yard that spanned two or three acres would have fit in fine in Beverly Hills.

Margo Sealock opened the door. "Richard," she said, smiling. She was wearing a gray turtleneck sweater and green pants and was barefoot. She smelled good, and he felt at ease at once. He stepped into a vaulted foyer where an imposing staircase curved up to an upper floor. She welcomed him, took his coat—a Green Bay Packers parka he found in Chachi's closet—and asked him if he found the place okay, fretted when he told her he missed his exit and had to turn around. She led him into the house, talking over her shoulder to him. "We can't thank you enough for doing this. I know how busy you must be." She offered him water, coffee, gave him a clearly oft-given tour of the house—its history and trivia. "The wood for this doorframe came from the hull of a sunken ship off the coast of Newfoundland." She was assured and sharp, a smiling conversationalist who, aside from her severe hair, presented herself conservatively as the astute, dynamic wife of a midwestern public official. She had that skill a lot of actresses had that made him feel like he had known her longer than he had, that could have almost convinced him they had more in common than they did.

"Has it been very hard being back here without Arthur around?" she said.

He did not answer right away.

She looked at him.

He said, "It's just strange to hear someone use his first name. The only one he ever allowed to do that was my mother."

"Oh," she said, "I'm sorry, I didn't mean to offend."

"No, no, it's not that—"

"I didn't know."

"There's nothing to know. It's okay."

"That's just what was printed on his invoices," she said. "He really was the best in the business." They came to a closed door. She knocked, opened it. Inside at a desk Martin Sealock looked up from documents he was bent over reading closely. He wore glasses that made him look older. A grin spread across his face. He took off his glasses and stood. "Richard's here," Margo told him. She turned to Richard. "I have to run, so I'll leave you to it. Do you have dinner plans? Would you join us this evening?"

"I would love to," Richard said, "but I can't—I have plans to meet some old friends at Arnold's."

"That sounds fun," she said. "I love Arnold's. I'm glad to see it's still hanging on. We need places like it in this town."

Sealock said, "Arnold's will be designated a historic landmark when I'm elected. First day in office."

Richard smiled. "You've got my vote. That is, if I had one."

Sealock laughed, gestured with his head. "Come in."

•   •   •

"I KNOW WHAT YOU'RE THINKING," SEALOCK SAID AFTER RICHARD autographed his LaserDisc copy of *Welcome to Henderson County* and they took a seat at the oak meeting table with crystal water pitchers and tumblers near the window overlooking a tennis court, a swimming pool, grass that was still more lush late in the fall than Richard could ever get his own yard, even in the peak of spring. "Populist candidate. Man of the people."

Richard laughed, arranging the pen, paper, and notes he'd brought with him. "It's not exactly the home I had imagined the champion of the working class would live in, no."

"Yeah, me neither. It's not me. It's Margo. Her family's one of those *families*, you know? The kind that can trace themselves to the original settlers and has a coat of arms. This is pretty average for them. If it were me? We'd be in a raised ranch out in Cudahy. That's more my speed. That's how I grew up. Here, they're scandalized if they catch you mowing your own lawn."

"Pretty good schools though, I bet."

"The public elementary school, where my eleven-year-old goes? Number one in the state. He's in fifth grade and writing papers on *Catcher in the Rye*. When I was his age I was shaking my teacher awake because she'd passed out at her desk. Every kid should get an education of the quality that Martin Jr. is getting. Not just kids whose parents have caught the breaks. My administration's going to make sure of it."

"You grew up here?"

"Illinois. Southeastern Illinois, almost Indiana. It was a similar kind of town as this one. Good people. Hardworking. There was a steel plant. Everyone's dad worked there. Mine did too, until we lost him."

"Oh, I'm sorry."

"Cancer. I was eleven. Mom did the best she could after that—cleaning rooms at the motel, working the cash register at the grocery store. But there were three of us kids. It was tough. One year we moved apartments four times. Makes you appreciate a home like this." He continued, "But that's why Fonzie and I got along so well, I think. We were kindred spirits. Always outsiders. What's the Dylan line? 'Always on the outside of whatever side there was.'"

"That should be your campaign slogan," Richard joked.

Sealock laughed. "We'll change it. Election's a week away? Sure."

"I want to use this," Richard said. "Everything you're talking about, that's what your commercial should be. You're sitting here, talking to me, telling me about this *upbringing*. Your opponent is this stodgy, boring old guy, right? You're the human. You're the hero."

Sealock glanced away, not quite willing to accept such adulation. "I am able to help the working people in ways Johnson cannot because he never was one."

"You're also energetic, young—"

"I'm forty-five."

"Forty-five is *young*," Richard said.

"How old are you?"

Richard shrugged and said, "Forty-five."

Sealock leaned back and clapped once, grinning. Richard was looking over Sealock's shoulder at a mounted and framed close-up photograph of a woman with her hair pulled tightly back, staring into the camera, her gaze cold but intense, almost brutal. What was most startling was how warm and caring this same woman had been to Richard moments earlier.

"Is that a Helmut Newton?"

Sealock turned to look at it. "He took it in Paris, not long after Margo and I met."

"You met in Paris?"

"Evanston. We were undergraduates at Northwestern. I was work-study, slopping ladles full of chow in the dining hall. She'd come through my line. I fell in love with her as soon as I saw her. Like everyone else. But I had an advantage over the rest of them: cookies. I slipped her free chocolate chip cookies until she finally noticed I was alive. We dated, and I fell only more in love with her. But then she left. To model. She went all over the world—Paris, New York. Meanwhile, I moped my way through the rest of my degree like a lovesick fool, then continued on to Kellogg and got my MBA. I had a couple of jobs with investment firms in Chicago, but partly because I did not have Margo, I burned out pretty fast. I became disillusioned with what I was doing. You ever feel like that?"

Richard nodded.

"That's when junk bonds were coming along. I could see what a con the whole financial industry had become. It wasn't about fueling business, it was about the rich getting richer. So I came here to Milwaukee and started an advisory shop. I liked the idea of helping regular, working people grow their money, save enough for a house, their kids' education."

"Why Milwaukee?"

"Because that's where Margo was. She was supposed to do an Yves Saint Laurent campaign but turned it down. They wanted her to do some things she wasn't comfortable with. Then she moved back home. I wasn't the least bit surprised when I heard about it. Margo was never one of these high-maintenance fashion models—she's a midwestern girl. Nor was I surprised when she took a job at a barely solvent homeless outreach organization here. She had that place turned around within a year and almost making a *profit*." He smiled. "They would have had to change their filing status. And man, *Yves Saint Laurent*? That thing would have made her a star. She could have had the world. But she wanted Milwaukee."

"I can see why you fell in love with her."

"A woman like Margo, you go to the ends of the earth for. If you get the chance to love her, you do whatever you have to do to make her yours, it doesn't matter what."

Richard wanted to ask, Like what, what do you mean? But he could barely keep up—he was scribbling notes so fast he did not know if he would be able to decipher them later. Sealock watched him, amused. "This is great stuff," Richard said, "this is really great. I didn't even have to bother coming up with these questions here." He tapped them with his pen then resumed writing.

Sealock said, "Johnson ran a new ad last night. Did you see it?"

"I was having trouble falling asleep. It helped."

"Exactly. I don't want to do what Johnson is doing. Talking into the camera, droning on. I don't want to be just another politician on TV talking at people. I need something that's going to grab them by the collar—their blue collar. You know what I mean?"

"Yes," Richard said.

"Something that inspires them to get out there and *vote*. Doesn't even have to be for me. Just to *vote*. Of course it would be nice if it was for me, but . . ." He smiled.

"I know exactly what you mean."

"I don't even want a *commercial*. I want a film. A thirty-second short film. Like that Apple commercial from the Super Bowl—you see it? *1984*, Big Brother on the screen, woman runs in and throws the hammer, shatters him?"

"It will be tough pulling off something of that scale with our time frame. When do you need this to air?"

"Friday night, during prime time. Maximum audience."

"Okay, well, whatever you do, you'll have to shoot it tomorrow and cut it on Thursday. You'll need a film crew who could do it—"

"I have one. We've used them for other stuff. They're good. But what about all your other projects?"

"What do you mean?"

"You have time today to write this thing? You probably need to get back to LA, get back to your other projects, right?"

"Well," he lied, "I *am* working on a few things."

"Yeah?" Sealock said, leaning forward. His eyes had become wide and bright. "What are they? As your number one fan."

"They're, you know, things in various stages of development."

"Yeah?" Sealock waited for more.

"Yeah." Richard shifted his weight. He remembered the lie he had told Potsie and Ralph at the bar. Then he said, "Actually, no. That's not true. To be honest? Aside from your commercial, I'm not working on much of anything."

Sealock didn't understand. "But you should be. Why not? You're a great writer. You have an Oscar nomination."

"It's a ruthless town. An Academy Award nomination from a decade ago is worth as much as having found a sticker in a box of Cracker Jacks. I'm barely hanging on out there."

He had never said that out loud to anybody before—not to his mother, not even to Lori Beth. He was too proud to be completely honest with them. But he needed to tell somebody. In Sealock he recognized the same drive he had, the same feeling of *otherness*.

Since he had been back, everyone had treated him like an intruder. Even talking to Al at the memorial service he had a feeling of distance, unease, like he could imagine Al was hiding years of bitter thoughts about him for leaving. He and Sealock both knew what it was like to be underestimated, written off, and to still have the ambition, the gall to keep going anyway. He told Sealock about *Suttree* and the dreams he had for directing the picture but how no one would let him do that because he did not have any experience and how he needed to raise five million dollars to make the film himself. And he told Sealock about Gleb's ultimatum.

"Here's an idea," Sealock said. "This ad? Don't just write it—direct it."

"Yeah?"

"You say you need experience, right? This will give you some."

Richard smiled at the thought. His directorial debut. He would do a fantastic job. It would win Sealock the election. The nation would notice. It would show them all that Richard Cunningham could produce work that compels and influences without compromising his aesthetic integrity. He would show it to financiers when he pitches them *Suttree*. He would tell them, "See? I've done it. I can do it. I *am* doing it." And they would give him everything he needs.

Sealock reminded him of Fonzie. They had the same inspiring effect on people. With just a few words, they could make you feel like you could do anything.

• • •

HE TURNED OFF THE ENGINE AND STEPPED OUT. IT WAS A CLEAR
day. He could see very far—all of Milwaukee lay out before him
in a panorama. They had chosen a fine location as their teenage
make-out spot, he had to admit. Tree trunks still bore bright,
freshly carved initials. It made him happy to see that young ro-
mantics were still coming to Inspiration Point.

They had tried to shut this place down once. The city planning commission wanted to bulldoze it to make way for an ex-
pressway off-ramp. The head of the commission was Howard
Cunningham. He was in favor of the off-ramp. It would be good
for business, would bring more customers to the store. The city
would make a lot of money. Richie and Fonzie led the teenagers
of Milwaukee in a protest against the brutalization of hallowed
ground. Richie painted signs and held a sit-in. Fonzie chained
himself to a boulder. At the public hearing before the commission
was to vote, Richie appealed to them in the name of romance.
He zeroed in on his father, scolding him, beseeching him like he
was some wicked, faceless public official. "Do you have a family,
sir?" he asked, his voice filled with indignation the way it can only
when we are young.

"I have a lovely wife, a beautiful daughter, and a smart-aleck
son," Howard said.

"Could you please tell us how you came to buy your house?"
Richard asked.

"Oh, come on, Richard, you've heard this story a million times," Howard said.

"Please, for the commissioners."

"Well, we found this house and we weren't quite sure whether we could buy it. Your mother was excited about it and I didn't quite know whether I could afford it. So we just went and talked it over."

"Where?"

"Where what?"

"Where did you go to talk it over?"

"Well, we drove up to . . ."

"Up to where, Dad?"

"Inspiration Point."

"I rest my case, Dad." The crowd of mostly pro-Inspiration Point supporters behind him cheered.

Howard called them to order. He realized what Inspiration Point meant to him. What it meant to everyone in that room and in that town. He said, "I've just been reminded, and pretty cleverly I would say, that there are more important things than business." He urged the commission to vote against the off-ramp. They did—they realized that they too had made their biggest life decisions there. It was the most popular place to propose in town, to see the fireworks on the Fourth of July. In the end, nobody wanted to live in a Milwaukee with no Inspiration Point. It was essential.

Richard now stepped to the edge of the ridge to take in the view. Something down on the dirt road made his skin tighten. It was a figure, idling on a motorcycle. He had one boot on the ground, propping himself up, and was looking up at Richard through the tinted visor of a black helmet, the same kind Fonzie used to wear for his jumps. It could have been Fonzie. The bike had a silver gas tank, no front fender, and ape-hanger handlebars—just like what Richard remembered Fonzie riding. The way the rider sat on it too even looked a little like Fonzie— same upright-and-back posture to his shoulders. But of course it was not Fonzie. Fonzie was gone. Richard waved, but the rider must not have been looking at him after all because he did not wave back. He revved the engine, lifted his boot onto the foot peg, and tore off.

Soon the sound of the engine faded.

Richard sat on the hood of his rental car with his notepad and tried to sketch out a script for the commercial. But he could not focus. All he could think about was what his father had said that day so long ago when Richie and Fonzie had saved this place. *There are more important things than business.*

It might have been a hundred years since he had said it. The world was no longer the world. But one thing had not changed: you still did whatever you had to do, became whatever you had to become, in order to come through for your family. He wondered what his father would have said about Gleb Cooper's offer. What would he say if he took it? Would he still call him an artist? He could hear his voice like he was here. "There *are* more important things than business. But there's nothing more important than your family."

• • •

"A MODEL WHO GAVE IT ALL UP FOR MILWAUKEE," SAID POTSIE.
"I don't believe it."

They were in the parking lot outside Arnold's, not long after night had fallen, sitting on barstools they had carried out. They were looking out onto the street, at the Bennigan's on the other side of it.

"I can," said Ralph. "What does Milan or Paris have that Milwaukee doesn't? I mean, we have Orange Julius."

"She has that Jackie O thing," Richard said. "Gracious, you know. Smart. But that hair. It's just enough rock and roll to let you know she's human."

"You should put her in the commercial."

"I thought about it. But Sealock says she's done being in front of cameras."

"How's she going to handle being first lady?" Potsie said.

Ralph made a strange high-pitched animal noise and straightened. "Here we go." He slowly rose from his stool. "We got action." A minivan was coming over from the overcapacity Bennigan's lot, entering the Arnold's lot, looking to steal one of the many open spots there. Ralph handed Potsie his can of Shotz.

"Get 'em," Potsie said.

Ralph began in a slow trot then screamed and broke into a crazed sprint toward the minivan. His arms flailed. He kicked his feet in the air. He sounded like a caveman. The minivan braked, backed out, and sped away. Ralph gave chase for a short distance then held up his arms in victory. He came back winded.

Richard watched the Bennigan's. There had to be eleven cars for each one at Arnold's. "You guys do this often?"

"We regulars all have shifts. Ours is Tuesday."

"It's a service to the community," Ralph said. "Plus Al gives us free fries."

"Why not just put up a sign or something?"

"This is more effective. More personal. Nothing's personal nowadays. It's all signs."

Potsie said, "What *are* you going to do for the commercial, Richard?"

"I don't know. I've got nothing."

"What's the problem?"

"It's got to be really good. It's got to be great. I don't have any ideas that are good enough. I don't even know where we're going to shoot it."

Potsie said, "Here's an idea. Why not shoot it at Sackett-Wilhelm?"

"Think they would let me?"

"You? No, of course not. But if you happened to know somebody very powerful there. Somebody very intelligent and good-looking, say, in quality control."

Ralph said, "Potsie can get the operations folks to go for it, absolutely. They'd do anything to get Sealock elected. We all would."

"Perfect," Richard said.

A car was coming over from across the street. Potsie and Ralph stood, but Richard stopped them. "No, no, no," he told them, putting his arms out to keep them back. He stood and took a step forward. "This one's mine."

It began as a growl. He felt the wind on his face, on his teeth, he heard his voice as the growl became a roar, and his arms swung on either side of him like propellers. The idea came all at once, as he ran. It was total but simple. It felt like a miracle. His whole body came alive with it. He did not know what to do with an idea so vast yet so brief being in his body like this. So he flailed and hollered and grunted until the driver turned around and sped away.

"Who's the lunatic?" Potsie was saying happily as Richard returned. He held out the basket of free fries.

Ralph wasn't saying anything, just smiling at him. He held out his hand. "Congratulations," he said.

"I have to make a call," Richard said, taking a fry, going inside to the pay phone. He dialed the direct line Sealock had given him.

He answered on the third ring.

"Meet me first thing tomorrow morning at Sackett-Wilhelm," Richard told him. "Bring your film crew. You want something that will grab them? What I have in mind will grab them and never let go."

• • •

THEY CHASED AWAY A FEW MORE CARS, THEN POTSIE AND RALPH had to leave, to be up early for work. Richard had an early start also. He stopped in the bathroom on his way out. As he stood at the trough, his eye went to the wall. Beneath his "Long Live the Fonz" from yesterday was a new message:

RC: Sit on It
–TJ

Every generation has its brush-offs. Gag me with a spoon was his daughter's. His had been *sit on it.* He hadn't said it or heard anyone else say it since about 1965. He had hardly even thought about it since high school. Everybody had said it then. He took a closer look. RC was him. But who was TJ? He tried to remember someone with those initials but could not.

He exited the bathroom, looked around for who might be TJ. At the bar were the Sackett-Wilhelm guys from yesterday. The one who had accused him of being a Madonna enthusiast looked over his shoulder at him. They met eyes. The guy smirked then turned back around.

"Real funny, *TJ,*" he muttered as he passed the guy on the way out the door. The guy looked at him but did not say anything. As the door closed behind him, Richard heard snickering.

He was a mile from the house, the only one on the road, when in the darkness behind him, in his rearview mirror, a single head-light appeared. It grew brighter and brighter. Came up close be-hind him and stayed there, filling the car with light, reflecting off the mirror into his eyes. "Okay, buddy, okay," Richard said, put-ting a hand up to block it. He rolled the window down and waved at the biker to pass, but the guy did not, he only pulled closer.

Richard brought his arm back inside the car and did not know what to do.

TJ, he thought. Local crazy. Nothing better to do but put in days at Sackett-Wilhelm then nights at the bar at Arnold's, get-ting loaded, then getting on his bike and looking for a fight.

He started putting it together. The biker earlier at Inspiration Point who reminded him of Fonzie.

What it meant was there were some here who did not only resent him—they wanted him out of town.

He held his breath and drove.

TJ disappeared from his rearview then reappeared on his left flank, passing him in the other lane. Richard got a good look. He looked twice. The first look, he felt the same thing he had felt at Inspiration Point. Silver gas tank, ape-hanger handlebars, no front fender. The way he rode. It was Fonzie, in that first look. But in the second look, there was logic and rationality, and there was a helmet—and it was not Fonzie. And the rider was leaning forward and ducking his head, and the engine grew suddenly louder, taking him away into the night, where he soon disap-peared along with the roar.

Richard pulled into the driveway and turned off the engine. He had calmed down by explaining the situation to himself. Of course the bike wasn't Fonzie's. That thing was gone—smashed up on a police impound lot somewhere. What was the rational explanation? What had *really* happened? Not much. A guy on a motorcycle that looked like Fonzie's had passed him on the road. It was nothing. There were a lot of bikers out this time of year. Maybe his grief was making him take things that had nothing to do with him—for example, some motorcycle enthusiast with the same taste as Fonzie's getting his last day of riding in before winter forced him to garage his bike until spring—and twist them until they became something that reminded him of Fonzie. Maybe this TJ was not harassing him at all, and maybe no one was—maybe Richard just missed his friend and wished he were here.

INSIDE THE HOUSE THE LIGHT ON THE ANSWERING MACHINE WAS blinking again.

"Richard!" Gleb Cooper said. "I'm at Dan Tana's with our friend. I'm talking about the *prince*. Listen, I floated the idea of you directing this thing. He *loves* it. You want a directing job? You got one. It's *yours*. The *choice* is yours. This is the opportunity of a lifetime. This kind of thing doesn't *happen*, Richard. All you have to do is tell me *yes*, like a *sane human being*. So call me back and tell me *yes*. By Saturday, Richard. *Saturday!*"

WEDNESDAY

THE SACKETT-WILHELM FACTORY WAS THE SIZE OF AN airport and just as busy. Shuttle buses delivered loads of workers from several satellite parking lots. It was approaching the time for a shift change, and a heavy crowd of workers was arriving. They were dignified and proud, content to have work waiting inside for them.

Potsie had arranged parking at the loading area, for easier access. A small film crew waited for Richard as he arrived with doughnuts. Lighting guy, camera guy, sound guy. Potsie and Ralph were there too. The crew's rusted old Ford Econoline van was parked nearby. They were blowing into their hands or drinking from fat Styrofoam cups of coffee, the steam rising out into the air around them. They were young—college, Richard guessed, or just out of it. Long hair, beanies. Mostly the production company they worked for did weddings, school pageants, and corporate training videos. It probably beat working at Kinko's. Richard went around shaking hands, introducing himself.

"Richard Cunningham," the sound guy said, squinting at him thoughtfully. "Where do I know that name?"

The lighting guy snapped his fingers and pointed at Richard, kind of leaning back and bending his knees. "*Sorority Slaughterhouse.*"

The sound guy turned to the lighting guy. "*Sorority Slaughterhouse?*"

"*Sorority Slaughterhouse.*"

They looked at Richard. "Tell me that was you," said the sound guy. "*Please.*"

"It was me," Richard confessed, dying a little inside.

They put their hands up and cheered, as if for a touchdown. The sound guy took Richard's hand in his. "Sir? Mr. Cunningham? It's an *honor* to work with you."

"Thank you," Richard said.

As the two explained to the camera guy the lowbrow pleasures of the no-budget horror movie with the enthusiasm of kids, Potsie said to them, "If you guys think that one's good, you should see *Welcome to Henderson County.* It's his masterpiece."

Richard turned to Ralph. "How high can you get me on your crane?"

"As high as you need."

A black Town Car arrived, pulling into the loading area and delivering Sealock in a suit.

"Ready for my close-up," he said.

Richard stepped forward to greet him. "We're just about all set, Martin—"

Sealock put his arm around his shoulder and turned him around to face the others. "Everybody, I can't thank you enough for your help here today. Before we start, I just wanted to take a second to recognize what a special moment this is. You will tell your grandkids about this day. Because today marks the directorial debut of the great Richard Cunningham, native son of Milwaukee and my favorite new filmmaker."

He shook Richard's hand and wished him good luck as the others applauded, and then they all went inside.

RICHARD SAT BACK AND TURNED OFF THE PLAYBACK ON THE editing bay that the sound guy, who was also the editing guy, had shown him how to use before departing the production company office and leaving Richard to it. His back hurt, his shoulders ached. His eyes were red and dry. He took a look at his watch—ten o'clock. He had been at it all day and evening, since the factory. It was Halloween—he had hoped to make it back to Joanie's early enough to hand out candy to trick-or-treaters, but he had had to miss it. His storyboards were in a trash can somewhere in the Sackett-Wilhelm factory. He hadn't needed them.

There were only two shots in the commercial. He had a dozen different versions of Sealock delivering his lines. The guy could act. He took direction more effectively than some actors Richard had known. Whatever he threw at him, Sealock would find new nuances in the words Richard had written for him, discovering different angles. He told the candidate after the shoot that if the election next Tuesday did not go well he might have a job for him on an embarrassing *Star Wars* knockoff.

The crew had come through. The camera was steady, the lighting was naturalistic, the audio was clear. Richard found he could read the crew well and hone his direction to their personalities, to get the best from them and make them want to give it to him. He had felt capable and talented. He wanted to keep going—direct *more*. He *could* keep going. For the first time since he could remember, he felt sure he had a future.

Richard tried different versions of the commercial, swapping in the different takes, until little by little—almost frame by frame—the finished film began to emerge.

He knew it was happening because it felt like somebody was leaving the room, pulling the door closed behind them, taking with them noise and endless impossible questions and ceaseless demands and an energy that was restless, gnawing. He kept working, working, waiting to hear, to *feel* the click of the door latch catching.

When it happened, he felt a calm descend over him, then that sadness that follows completion of a project, that kind that should have its own word. Then the second-guessing. He looked at the clock. He played it back one last time. Fortunately, time and fatigue would keep him from continuing to fuss with it. It was done. Time to let it go.

It was too late to deliver it to the local network stations—that could wait until morning. He had changed his return flight to Friday morning, to allow for any necessary reshoots or problems. Richard had invited Sealock to come to the production company office to see the final edit before it went out, but Sealock's schedule did not allow for it.

"I trust you," he had said in the factory parking lot as the crew packed up following the shoot. "Just make me look good." He smiled.

"I hope it gets you elected," Richard said.

"And I hope it helps get you back to where you ought to be," Sealock said. They shook hands and said goodbye.

THURSDAY

RICHARD LOOKED THROUGH CHACHI'S CLOSET. HE NEEDED something to wear—he had packed for only a few days and there had not been time to do laundry. He found a flannel shirt and jeans. He and Chachi had a similar enough waistline, and he would roll up the too-short sleeves of the shirt. But they had different shoe sizes, so Richard had to stay with the Bruno Maglis.

The morning was spent delivering copies of the commercial to the network stations. The campaign had already paid for the airtime, but at each station the person in charge of such things had to screen the commercial first before accepting it. At the third station, the guy told Richard after it was over that he had never seen anything like it, that it had changed the way he was going to vote: Sealock, all the way.

When Richard left the final station and got back into the Tempo to find somewhere for lunch, the feeling of a job well done quickly gave way to a rapidly spreading melancholy. It spilled across his consciousness like the colors at sunset. He realized he had no real reason to be here in his hometown anymore. It was time to start saying goodbye.

As he drove he passed a junkyard. It looked like it had been there a long time. Richard had driven past it before, but he had never really noticed it. There was something immediately inside the fence out front that caught his attention. He made a U-turn, pulled in to the parking lot, and got out of the car. The sign above the junkyard read: TJ'S AUTO PARTS AND SALVAGE.

A small trailer outside the fence served as the office. It was plastered with old license plates and signs for VALVOLINE and SI-MONIZE.

He went to the chain-link fence, topped with barbed wire, that surrounded the property, put one hand on the links, and bent to look. It was smashed up. Mangled. Hardly stood upright on its kickstand. It had been such a long time since he had seen it, but it did not matter—he knew it. This was Fonzie's motorcycle.

The trailer door swung open. Two large, slobbering Rottweilers came down the steps. A man in coveralls who Richard had never seen before appeared in the doorway behind them. For a moment he watched Richard backing away from the dogs, then said, "They won't hurt you if you don't hurt them." Richard stood still, not so sure. One of the dogs sniffed his hand then lost interest, went to a fence post, and raised his leg.

"You need something?" said the guy.

"This motorcycle," Richard said, pointing to it. "Where'd it come from?"

"Who's asking?"

"I'm Richard Cunningham. From Los Angeles, California. That's my friend's bike."

"It is, is it?"

"Yeah. Fonzie. Arthur Fonzarelli."

The man relaxed. "Any friend of Fonzie's," he said. He came down the stairs, came toward Richard holding his hand out. "TJ Parker," he said.

"TJ," Richard said.

"That's what I said. Fonzie was my friend too."

"How'd you get it?"

"Police. They let me haul away the wrecks nobody claims."

Richard winced. "I hate thinking of his bike as that."

"Me too. That's why I made extra sure to get it as soon as they'd give it to me. It's awful what happened."

"Yes it is." It was quiet. TJ didn't know what more to say. He turned to the motorcycle.

"This bike is something special. A 1949 Triumph Trophy TR5 Scrambler Custom with the castrator tank rack removed, bullet-holed muffler modified to a pea-shooter, front fender yanked off, ape hangers bolted on, gas tank painted chrome, vintage all-alloy engine on a 11198T frame. Nothing there it doesn't need. Yeah, this is Fonzie's bike all right."

"How'd you know him?"

"He came by now and again to pick up parts for his shop. Fonzie didn't talk a lot. But when he did, it was about one thing. Automobiles. That was fine by me. I never knew anyone who knew so much about them. I can't believe he went out the way he did."

"I know what you mean."

"But there's still something about it that keeps bugging me."

"What's that?"

"It's nothing, probably. The last few months, I started seeing him a little more often. He'd come around sometimes not even looking for parts—he'd come just to shoot the breeze. He seemed to be in a real good mood, real happy. But last time I saw him? Probably a week before he died? He was even more quiet than ever. Wouldn't even talk carburetors with me. I asked him what it was. He said nothing. But I could tell something serious was on his mind. The guy looked like he had the weight of the world on his shoulders. When I heard the news, know what my first thought was? That it must have had something to do with what had been on his mind that day."

"TJ, did you write me a message on the wall at Arnold's?"

"I haven't been to Arnold's in years."

It didn't make any sense. Why would someone leave that message for him? To lead him here? But why?

"Could I get inside the fence? Take a closer look at it?"

"I suppose so." TJ opened the gate, and the dogs rushed past. TJ followed, then Richard behind him.

"God," said Richard, looking at it.

"That's what crashing at seventy, eighty miles an hour will do."

"It really happened, didn't it," Richard said. "It really did. I don't think I really understood until now, seeing this." He and TJ stared at the bike in silence. It felt like Fonzie's grave site. One of the dogs was sniffing it, like he knew it was the focus of attention.

Then Richard had a revelation. *Sit on it.* Maybe he had misunderstood and it wasn't an insult, or even a reference to their youth. It was an instruction. He took a step forward and swung one leg over the seat, got on. "Careful," said TJ, "it's not stable." He lifted his feet, put them on the foot pegs. He took hold of what remained of the ape-hanger handlebars. It was a mistake. He didn't like it. It felt like a violation, a trespassing. But more than that—the bike could not hold his weight. The kickstand gave out and it fell. "Whoa," TJ said, reaching out to grab Richard's arm to keep him from falling with it. Richard got his feet under him and stood, but the bike was already down, sending the curious dogs leaping back. He stood straddling it, looking down at it. TJ helped him step away.

"It's all just barely hanging together," TJ said. "You okay?"

"Yeah, yeah. Thanks. Can you help me stand it back up?"

"Grab that end," TJ said, pointing toward the rear. "I'll take the front."

Richard reached down then stopped. "What's that?" He could have seen it only at this angle.

"What's what?"

"That blue paint. See it? Right there." Richard pointed at the bottom of the rear fender, and TJ leaned in toward it, squinting. "And the way it's bent right there at the bottom. Kind of looks like someone hit it or something," Richard said. "Doesn't it?"

"Sure does," said TJ, bending over it. "That man took care of his bike. The word *obsessed* doesn't do it. He wouldn't have been riding around with a ding like that. No way. Almost looks like he got clipped from behind."

Richard said, "Think he was?"

TJ thought about it for a moment. Then he said, "No. No way. Cops would have considered that."

Richard said, "Yeah. They would know." They were quiet. Then Richard said, "How would they though?"

"Well," said TJ, "because they're cops. They know that kind of thing. They investigate. If a bike was clipped, well, they know that. They *see* that." He added, impatiently, "They're cops."

Richard said, "No, yeah, you're probably right." He thanked TJ for his time and waved goodbye to the dogs. He got back in the car and drove off, but he couldn't stop thinking about it. He had to know for sure. He turned around, headed toward downtown to the Milwaukee Police Department.

• • •

"I'D LIKE TO SEE KIRK," RICHARD TOLD THE DESK SERGEANT sitting behind the dirty, nearly opaque bulletproof glass reading the *Sporting News*. On the cover was the kid from UNC who had hit the winning jump shot in the 1982 NCAA championship game against Georgetown, Richard remembered. The Next Dr. J, said the *Sporting News*. Richard had his doubts. No one would ever be better than Dr. J. And that included this kid, Michael Jordan.

"Do you have an appointment?" the cop asked without looking up.

"Well," Richard said, "no, but—"

"Then you may have a seat."

"It's about Arthur Fonzarelli."

The desk sergeant looked up and said, "Fonzarelli?"

"That's right."

The desk sergeant stood and went in the back. When he returned he did not look at Richard. "He'll be right with you," the desk sergeant said.

Richard waited, thinking about the first time he had ever been here. There had been a drag race, out by the airport. Fonzie against some greaser named Skizzy Scarlik. They chose Richard to drop the white flag to begin the race, because everyone could trust he would be fair. Fonzie giving him such a job was a major responsibility. It signaled a profound upgrade in social status. His father would not let him go, but he snuck out of the house to make it there. Howard noticed he was gone and came looking for him. Kirk and the cops came, arrested everyone who was there—even Howard.

The desk sergeant's phone rang, and he waved Richard up. He hit a buzzer, and the bulletproof glass door unlocked and Richard opened it and went through.

The desk sergeant escorted him back, down a little hallway, past a break room. And then they rounded a corner and he found himself in a big, open, busy room. Cops in uniform leaned on corners of desks, sorting through documents. Other cops sat half-hidden in cubicles with phones to their heads. It was loud with the clacking of typewriters and shrill ringing of telephones.

He found Kirk at a desk in the corner, out in the open with all the others.

"Lieutenant Kirk, my name is—"

"I remember you, Cunningham," Kirk said, not looking up from his paperwork. "I almost didn't recognize you the other day leaving the funeral home. You used to have the bright red hair. Not anymore, huh?"

Richard was fifteen years old again. Coming up empty for words. Insecure, anxious.

"What's this about Fonzarelli?" Kirk said with no patience. His finger was tapping on his desk and he was looking all around the room, anywhere but at Richard. He never even made eye contact with him.

Richard told him about the junkyard—the motorcycle and the blue paint. "I guess I was wondering, is it possible something else happened that night? Other than what we think?"

Kirk looked down at his paperwork. He breathed heavily through his nose, almost snorting like a warthog. He didn't answer.

Richard said, "Well? Is there?"

"No," Kirk said.

"But that blue mark. And the way the fender's bent."

"Have you been up to that bridge lately? You haven't. Know how I know? Because if you had, you'd see something there that might interest you. The guardrail is blue."

"You've tested it to make sure it's the same paint?" Richard asked.

"Yeah, we tested it. We used all the money and equipment we don't have."

"Okay, fine, forget the paint. What about the fact that it was on the rear fender? Why would the rear fender be banged in if Fonzie went headfirst into the guardrail?"

"You're suggesting I haven't done my job?"

"No, sir. I'm not suggesting that."

"I remember when you left. Everybody was happy for you. Going off and pursuing your dreams. I was happy too. Know why? One less punk I had to keep in line."

"I wasn't a punk."

"You all were."

109

"We were kids."

"You were a juvenile delinquent. I arrested you twice: once in 1956 for drag racing, then again in 1958 for violating curfew."

"That was an unjust curfew. It was completely arbitrary. You only set it because someone broke a window at the high school the night before and you couldn't figure out who it was. It wasn't legal. I was going to lead a demonstration against it—"

"Inciting a riot," Kirk said.

"—but then I got locked inside at Arnold's. To call for help on the pay phone, I had to break in to the jukebox for a dime. I'd almost got it open when you walked in."

"Caught you red-handed. Took you down for stealing—*and* for breaking my curfew."

"You sure did."

"Nothing but trouble."

"Nothing but a *kid*."

"Look. Just because you saw *paint* doesn't give me cause to reopen the investigation. The case is closed. Go home. Go back to Hollywood, lay by your pool. Leave the real work to the real people."

Richard raised his voice. "Why won't you take this seriously? What's your problem?"

The room fell silent. All the cops on the floor were watching.

Kirk was looking at him now. "You want to know what my problem is? Read the morning paper. Yesterday we pulled in a guy with an Uzi and a trunkful of heroin. An *Uzi*. *That's* my problem. A no-good, over-the-hill greaser who had it coming? Who thought the rules didn't apply to him? And had to find out the hard way that they do? That's *not* my problem."

Richard's lip trembled. His hands curled into fists. "Take it back," he said.

"Want to visit your old jail cell, Cunningham? That can be arranged." He called out, "Sauer!" An officer in uniform arrived. Early thirties. Kirk said, "Get this guy out of here before he does something he regrets."

Sauer took Richard gently by the arm. "Come on," he said. There was kindness in his voice. Like he knew well how impossible Kirk could be. Richard turned and went with him.

As he led him back the way he came, Officer Sauer said, "It's not you. Since June, he's been acting like there's a nail stuck in the bottom of his shoe."

"And how's that different from usual?"

Sauer chuckled. "Not different. Just worse. It's this election. The governor's got Kirk's head in a vise about keeping big crime stories out of the papers through election day. He's afraid Sealock will use it to make him look like crime is running amok on his watch. That heroin we picked up yesterday is exactly the kind of thing he has in mind—and the papers are already running with it. Meanwhile, he's got the big boys here riding him to make more arrests, bigger and more spectacular ones so we look better. If Sealock is elected, he'll be taking a hard look at budgets— ours included. So Kirk's getting it from all sides." He led Richard through the lobby and opened the door for him. "By the way," he said, "I'm sorry about your friend."

Richard thanked him and left.

HE HAD FORGOTTEN ABOUT LUNCH BUT HE WAS NO LONGER hungry. As he drove he felt like inside of his head were the ends of two pipes that did not meet; they were an inch apart, and he could not figure out how to join them, so both just dripped and dripped.

They dripped and dripped on his way to Sealock's house.

He went there without calling ahead, hoping to catch him. He had not planned on seeing Sealock again. They had said their goodbyes. But he didn't know who else to talk to about this.

It was a straight northern shot up to Whitefish Bay, up I-794 to the Lincoln Memorial Drive split, which went along the beach, and he rode that up all the way past the University of Wisconsin–Milwaukee until it tucked back inland. The horizon was endless, and Lake Michigan looked like the ocean.

When he got to Sealock's street, there were black official-looking cars in the driveway. Richard rang the doorbell. Church bell–like chimes rang out inside.

"Richard," said a woman's voice behind him. Margo Sealock was coming around from the side of the house. "I didn't think we'd see you again. Is everything okay with the commercial?"

"Is he here?" he said.

"You look ill. What's the matter?"

"Nothing. I mean, I don't know exactly. He's inside?"

"He's on the phone with his press team, putting together a statement about the drug bust." She read his face. "It's urgent, isn't it. I'll let him know you're here."

As she stepped onto the porch she lost her footing on the edge of the first step and stumbled. He reached out and caught her by the elbow. She laughed at herself.

"You're okay?" he said.

"Fine," she said. She put her hand on the doorknob then stopped and turned to face him. She said, "You know, I'm glad you're here. I was hoping to talk to you about something."

The door opened and Sealock appeared in the doorway. "Richard," he said, surprised.

Richard looked back to Margo. "What did you want to tell me, Mrs. Sealock?"

"Nothing," she said. "Just—I hope you'll show him for who he is."

Richard was moved at her protectiveness for her husband. "Don't worry, Mrs. Sealock. That's what I absolutely intend to do."

IN SEALOCK'S OFFICE, RICHARD STOOD IN THE MIDDLE OF THE room. Drip, drip, drip went those pipes in his head.

That dent on the rear fender. That blue paint. Kirk.

Sealock said, "What's up, Richard?"

"It's Fonzie."

"Fonzie?"

"Yeah. It's all just not sitting right with me."

"What do you mean?"

"I dropped off the commercial at the stations—"

"Okay."

"—and on the way back I passed this junkyard. Called TJ's. Do you know it? Fonzie's bike was there."

"*Fonzie's* was?"

"Yeah."

"You mean, his *bike*-bike?"

"Yeah, the one he was riding when he, you know. It was just right there, right out in the open."

Sealook looked away, trying to process this. "Why was it there? Shouldn't it be in a police impound lot or something?"

"The cops let him have the unclaimed wrecks."

"Here. Take a seat." They sat down in the leather chairs. Sealock sat close to Richard. Their knees were almost touching. Sealock was thinking out loud. "I guess if it was an accident there's no reason for them to hold on to it any longer. Go on. Fonzie's bike at the junkyard."

"Right. Well, I took a look at it."

"At the bike."

"At the bike. And the darnedest thing. There was *blue* on

114

it. Like a streak of blue, on the back fender." It did not sound like much, Richard could hear it from Sealock's perspective. It sounded a little crazy, a little *yeah, so what?*

But Sealock understood. He was staring through Richard, processing this, seeing the importance of it. "Why was there blue?"

"Exactly."

"Fonzie wouldn't have been riding around with something like that on his bike."

"Yes. *Yes.* So I brought it to Kirk."

"The bike?"

"No, I mean I just *went* to Kirk. To tell him about it. You know, to help. And ask, you know, did they notice it and what did they think it was. Thinking, you know, it's nothing, but—"

"But he's your friend."

"He's my friend."

"You have to be sure, and you want to help."

"Right. Yeah."

"So what'd Kirk say?"

"He blew me off. He says the blue mark is from the bridge and that's all there is to it."

Sealock scrunched his nose. "From the *bridge?*"

"Yeah, he says Fonzie hit a blue spot on the bridge or something."

"That doesn't make much sense."

"Yeah."

"If that's what happened," Sealock said, "the blue should be on the front of the bike, not the back."

"Yeah. *Yeah*. And otherwise, it's perfect back there. Not a scratch."

Sealock had his hands on his hips. His face had become gray and heavy. "Kirk," he said, shaking his head, pulling on the bridge of his nose with the thumb and forefinger of his right hand.

Richard watched the man's back, the side of his face. Richard watched it closely because it was a gauge for how he himself should be feeling about all this. He wanted to know how he felt about this, and what he should do—and Sealock's reaction was paramount to that decision.

"Richard," Sealock said, "Kirk is a *hugely* important person in this city. And what you're suggesting . . ."

"I'm not suggesting anything."

"No, I think you are though."

Richard wondered: Was he?

"Tell me," Sealock said, "what exactly did Kirk have against Fonzie?"

Richard said, "Are you kidding? What did the Jets have against the Sharks?"

"Just hated him, huh?"

"*Hated* him."

"Was it something Fonzie did?"

"It wasn't what he did so much as who he was. Fonzie's very existence in this town was a living, breathing insult to Kirk.

Always undermining his authority. He was always the one guy Kirk could never quite touch. He was smarter than Kirk, faster than Kirk, and cooler than Kirk. And everyone knew it. No matter how far up the ladder Kirk climbed, it must have been like Fonzie was always still there, a constant reminder of just how small and meaningless Kirk was. And I'll bet that just humiliated him."

Sealock said, "Look, can I tell you something?"

"Yeah."

"No, I mean, something sensitive. Highly sensitive. That you can't tell anybody else. Ever."

Richard's pulse quickened. He was excited to share Sealock's confidence and have his trust.

Sealock said, "I don't really know how to say this. Look, don't get me wrong, okay? Kirk's an excellent cop—as far as we know, anyway. But I don't like him. I don't trust him. I never have."

"That makes two of us."

"He's been around too long, has become too entrenched, has too many allegiances—and unfortunately not all of them are to justice and the people's well-being. I think he lost sight of the purpose of the law and can only see the law. You know?"

"I do. Exactly. He's always been on some power trip."

"I want to shake up the top brass over at the police department once I'm elected. Get some fresh blood in there, enact some real, positive justice reform, some real change. Kirk knows that, I don't make any secret of it, it's part of my platform, I talk about it all the time. When I'm elected, he's out. And I'll see to it that his replacement reopens the investigation into Fonzie's death. We just need some evidence. Something firm. Maybe there's something at the crash site. Have you been out there yet, to the bridge?"

"I've been avoiding it."

"The cops could have overlooked something."

"Like what?"

"Could be anything—a clue someone who only knew Fonzie as well as you did would notice. It's a long shot, but why not take it? Otherwise, we don't have much to work with."

"I'll go now."

"Later might be better. When it's darker and there's less traffic."

"Yeah. Okay. Later."

Richard had not wanted things to go in this direction. But hearing the words come out of Sealock's mouth made him realize that things already had. They had already gone in this direction, way back at the police station, the minute Kirk blew him off. He had not wanted to admit it to himself. It was too big, too awful of a turn for an old rivalry to have taken.

When Richard left Sealock's house it had grown almost completely dark, but one fact had become completely illuminated: Lieutenant Kirk had something to do with Fonzie's death.

· · · ·

RICHARD PARKED THE TEMPO UNDER THE BRIDGE ON A LITTLE bank used for fishing. He stepped over discarded lures and empty Michelob bottles. He walked up the embankment. He had a flashlight from Joanie's. He kept it off for now. Up above, the stars in the dark sky watched him.

He stood at the guardrail and looked down at what Fonzie had seen as he died. A shimmering abyss. It was so dark he probably did not even see it approaching. Richard imagined it felt cold. That's the only way he knew it was coming. Only a few seconds. And then the cold and the darkness were everywhere, were everything. Maybe Fonzie kicked and fought, panicking. It was only natural. Or maybe he was cool. Either way, in the end it did not matter.

It was close to nine o'clock. There was no traffic. The city had gone home for the night. He threw his leg over the Jersey barrier and climbed over.

He walked along the shoulder forty or fifty feet until he came to the spot where Fonzie had crashed. He knew it was the place because of all the flowers people had placed there, and all the pocket combs, and little messages. The wreckage and debris had been cleaned up—even the shattered glass of the bike's headlight. There was nothing left. No evidence. No clues.

The flowers covered up most of the wall. He knelt down and turned on the flashlight. With his free hand he moved aside the flowers so he could see the rail. He put the flashlight on it and was disappointed to see blue. The rail was in fact blue. A long strip of blue, going the whole length of the bridge. And it was deep blue, the same shade as the streak on the bike, or at least close to it. There was a dent where Fonzie had hit. It looked small. Innocuous. The blue paint there was not even nicked.

"Hey," called a voice. He dropped the flashlight. He looked back. It was a cop, sitting inside a Milwaukee Police Department cruiser. "Cunningham," said the voice, "I've been looking all over for you, what the hell are you doing?"

It was Officer Sauer. He was leaning across the passenger seat from behind the wheel, looking confused through his rolled-down passenger window. He unbuckled his seat belt and opened the door, got out. Faced Richard over the hood, putting his arm on it. "You're not thinking of jumping are you?"

"No, no," Richard said, "I just hadn't been out here yet."

"Paying your respects?"

"Paying my respects, yeah."

"Good, because I don't want to have to call the search units again. It's been barely a week since the last time. I've been looking for you, I'm glad I found you: After you left, Kirk calmed down and thought more about what you were saying. He thinks you might be onto something about the paint. He wants to see you down at the station."

"He's there now?"

"Of course. He's Kirk. What do you think, he has a home or something? Where'd you park? Jump in. I'll give you a lift back to your car."

I was too hard on Kirk, Richard thought. *Of course he'd grown more sensible with age and rank. I would have seen that if I had given him more of a chance, if I hadn't let the grief make me paranoid.*

Richard picked up the flashlight. As he straightened, the light passed over the cruiser. The body panel of the front passenger side was smooth—except for one place, where it looked like a dent had been hammered out. It was right up front, near the headlight, right in the stripe of color that went lengthwise across the side of the car. The color of the stripe was blue. The same blue as the guardrail. In the place where the dent had been hammered out, the blue was just slightly darker. Like it had been recently repainted.

All the pleasantness disappeared from Sauer's face as he saw what Richard was looking at. He put his hand on the grip of his holstered gun. "Hands above your head." He came around the front of the car, keeping himself square to Richard. "Turn around and put your hands above your head."

Sauer was reaching behind his back for handcuffs when they heard it. A heavy, choking rumble. Richard was first to see the source of the sound: tearing toward them along the bridge from the distance was a single headlight. It was growing quickly. It was a solitary rider in a leather jacket sitting atop a silver motorcycle. Same helmet. Same leather jacket. Same bike. It was the biker from Inspiration Point. And it was the one who had followed him home from Arnold's. Richard glanced at Sauer.

He did not know what he was going to do. The rider's right hand pumped the grip, and the engine snorted and roared. The biker kept going right past but slammed a skid turn and came to a sudden stop, filling the air of the bridge with the stink of burned rubber. The engine idled, chortled. There was only one guy around there who had ever ridden like that. The jeans, the jacket, the bike—Sauer and Richard were both standing frozen in confusion and shock, trying to understand if they were seeing what they thought they were seeing—that is, *who* they were seeing. Finally Sauer said it:

"Fonzie?"

Fonzie waved to Richard to come on, jump on. Richard did not think about it—he ran, jumped onto the back of the motorcycle, and held on. Fonzie peeled out, putting more smoke between them and Sauer. Sauer raised his gun and fired into the cloud. Sparks flew as bullets ricocheted off the pavement before Fonzie and Richard. Over the bike's engine, the shots he fired sounded small and harmless as Richard and Fonzie sped off into the night.

THE PLANE FLEW ABOVE THE OCEAN, TOWARD HOME. IT WAS A homecoming—the first one. Richie and Ralph, two young men in green army uniforms, their faces still fleshy and formless despite the mustaches they had grown—the faces not of men but old boys. They were somewhere in between, above that ocean, even after the military. It did not seem to bother Ralph, but it bothered Richie. He had expected to feel differently at the end. To have a different face. When he had imagined this day, he had seen himself with a harder face, eyes that were more weary. He thought the army would have given him trials over which to triumph, darkness through which to persevere, a face of granite and steel. All it had given him was Greenland.

He had manned a desk, overseen an administrative supply cache. Unpacking boxes of staplers, tallying inventory of electrical cords. They gave him awards, commendations. His superior officer called him out in front of the whole unit: "The perfect soldier," he had called him, for taking his desk duties as seriously as those of a Special Forces captain. There was a growing conflict in Southeast Asia, but he had Lori Beth and his little boy living with him on the base. Even if he had put in for a transfer to infantry—which he would not, because he could not bear the thought of putting Richie Jr. at risk of losing his father—he would have been denied on those grounds. His country then was still so sure about its destiny, its righteousness. It was not yet desperate for bodies to throw at an already body-filled catastrophe, though soon it would be.

Marriage, fatherhood, service to his country—nothing he had tried to become a man had worked. All of it was vital, but none of it had done to him what he thought it would. None of it had given him the face. Only one thing would, he was beginning to understand. What was missing, he realized, on that plane, was him—he knew what he wanted to do, but he couldn't face it. So he had taken no bets on his own talents, his own wits. All he had done instead was be perfect.

Lori Beth and Richie Jr. were with him too on the plane. She was already beginning to show with Caroline. He never told her what the thing was he could not face: Hollywood. *Hollywood.* As they packed for home, for reentry into civilian life, Lori Beth talked with love about Milwaukee—its schools, which neighborhood they would live in, what Richie could do for work there. Her face glowed. He had said nothing, just smiled. He wanted to be who she wanted him to be. Who his kids needed him to be.

They all took a cab from the airport to the Cunningham house. Inside, his parents and sister went about another day without him, not knowing they all were back in the country, outside the door, and were home for good. Ralph said, looking out the car window, "We pulled it off. I was sure my mom would have let it slip that we'd been discharged. Man, they're going to flip."

Lori Beth went inside first with Richie Jr. Ralph and Richie listened to the shouts of joy as she closed the door behind her.

Ralph said, "I'm glad to be home. I'm never leaving again. How about you, Richie?"

"Yeah," Richie said, wishing to God he could mean it.

"Here we go," Ralph said, smiling. "Ready?" He opened the car door, headed up to the house. Richie paid the driver, got his duffel from the trunk, and hustled after. Ralph went inside to a new wave of happy shouting. Richie waited a moment, listening from outside. He heard them all: his father, his sister, he heard his overwhelmed mother say to Ralph, "But if you're out of the army, where's Richie?"

Lori Beth said, "Well, you know how the army tends to make little mistakes?"

"Yeah, like Korea," Ralph said. "Well, they've done it again. I'm afraid Richie had to stay back to—"

Richie opened the door and stepped inside, dropping his duffel. Never had he had a bigger smile. He spread his arms out wide, his heart growing, growing, close to bursting. He finished Ralph's sentence:

"Pay the cabdriver!"

His family fell on him, swallowed him up in their arms.

Then the kitchen door opened. Fonzie had heard it all from the garage apartment.

"Red!" he shouted. "*Red!*" He ran to Richie, put his arms around him. Richie did not know what to do with how happy he was to see his friend—so he lifted him off the ground.

He remembered the weight of the guy then. Not fat—Fonzie was never anything but fit as a drill sergeant—but substance.

Now with his arms around Fonzie again, holding on as they sped through the night, Fonzie seemed slight, almost frail. Middle age had not added the flesh and fat it had to the rest of them. The man must have lost several pounds this week, wherever he had been hiding out from Kirk and Sauer.

The icy wind pulled at Richard's face. It lashed at his arms. He was putting it all together. It *was* a hit-and-run. But more than that, it was a hit job. Sauer had tried to kill Fonzie. A *cop*. He ran him off the road. And Kirk was the one who had ordered it. But Fonzie had survived somehow and—and what exactly? Fonzie was weaving around cars, slamming through red lights, narrowly skirting oncoming traffic. They exited the interstate onto a little dark two-lane road. They were outside the city. At last they came to an intersection lit up brightly where Wisconsin Power was doing work on the road and had traffic blocked off and backed up. Fonzie had to slow down so they could get through the intersection, and Richard was able to shout through Fonzie's helmet and into his ear, "Where are we going?" No response. The engine roared again as they got through the intersection and Fonzie sped up once more.

They went deep into the country, the woods—somewhere around Sheboygan, Richard guessed. He kept looking up, expecting a sky full of police helicopters sicced on them by Kirk after Sauer radioed him with the news. It only got darker.

Richie had tried to resume the life he had lived before he and Ralph joined the army. He took a job his father got him. He and Lori Beth shopped for homes that had enough room. But within days he fell into a hole the likes of which he had never known and never would again. He was seeing his future—it consisted of two lines: one faded and one bright. The faded one was the one where he should have been. The bright one was the one where he was. And he couldn't connect them. But he knew he *should*, he *had* to. It was his obligation as a living being. But he felt like he never would. One day he could not go home—he stayed out all day, late into the night, drinking, feeling the despair that he would never be who he should. He was in a dive bar, alone and working on going out of his mind, when Fonzie walked in. He'd been all over the city, checking every bar for him. Fonzie tried to get him to come home. There was drunken rage. Richie took a swing—his sucker punch connected on the side of Fonzie's head. He knew at once the mistake he had made. But he did not apologize—he swung again. Fonzie dodged, pinned Richie down on the pool table.

"You're okay," he said into Richie's ear. He was almost cooing. It did not conceal his anger at being hit. He let Richie up. "You're okay," he said again.

"I can't live like this," Richie was saying. He was almost crying. "I can't go around living my life pretending I'm happy all the time. It's no good, Fonz."

"I know. I know. You've been living your life for everybody else. You've been the perfect son, the perfect student, the perfect father—"

"The perfect soldier."

"Perfect friend. Now's the time to take responsibility for your own life. You gotta do what you want to do, Richie."

"It's not that simple. Lori Beth has her heart set on living in Milwaukee."

"Lori Beth has her heart set on living the rest of her life with *you*. Don't sell her short. She'll back you on anything you want to do. We *all* will."

Richie knew he was right. But his being right meant that what Richie had to do would be hard. He had to finally turn and face that thing he couldn't: Hollywood. He said, "You're single. You don't know what it's like to have people depending on you each and every day."

"I'll be fair with you, okay? I *don't* have a wife and kids. But if I had *yours*—I wouldn't let *nothing* stop me."

"You know, if I decide to go out there, I know I can make it."

"There is no doubt in my mind. I'm already behind the movie theater, waiting to sneak in to see your first flick."

Days later, Richie's bags were packed again. He stood in a coat and tie in his parents' living room. Lori Beth and Richie Jr. waited for him out in the yard. Lori Beth had agreed that they had to give Los Angeles a chance. Fonzie had been right—she was all for it. She had been so enthusiastic about settling down in Milwaukee only because she thought it had been what Richie wanted. Richie had just told his parents and sister the news when Fonzie came through the door.

"Hey, Richie," the Fonz said, almost shouting, holding something in his hand. "I got 'em." He was energetic, almost as excited for Richie as Richie was. He slapped them against his palm then handed them to him. "First-class tickets to Tinseltown."

Richie took them, read them. "Fonz, I can't afford first class."

"Sure you can. It's on me. I got 'em from Yolanda down at the travel agency. One more date and you're going to Europe." He looked over his shoulder, out the open door, at everybody waiting. "Well," he said, growing serious, uncomfortable, "I guess this is it."

"Fonz, listen. I'm a writer. Or at least I hope so." He reached into his jacket pocket, took out a letter. "I wrote this to you this morning. Because I knew that when we were face-to-face like this, well, I might not be able to find the words." Fonzie tensed. His eyes locked on Richie. He looked almost angry, Richie thought. He looked almost the way he used to, before they were friends. His hands were in his pockets, and his shoulders were slack. He was quiet, his jaw grinding, his body twitching in that restless way it did, like he could never get comfortable. "How do you thank someone who's been everything to you?" Fonzie turned away, looking at the floor, like he didn't want to hear it, *couldn't handle* hearing it, but Richie kept going. "Your brother. Your protector. I just don't know how I could ever say that."

He looked back up at Richie and shrugged. "I think you just did."

Richie went to put the letter back in his pocket. But Fonzie reached out and took it from him. Looking Richie in the eyes, man to man, he put the letter to his chest.

"I just want to tell you," Fonzie said, whispering, struggling to get out the words. "That I love you. Very much."

Then, with one last look back, and still holding Richie's letter to his heart, Fonzie walked out the door and was gone, leaving Richie alone with nothing, just his whole life—and his family's— in his own hands.

• • •

BUT HIS FRIEND WAS NOT DEAD. HIS FRIEND WAS ALIVE. RICHARD could now tell him all the things he had never been able to say. And he could hear all the things Fonzie had never told *him*. He could not wait to hear about what had happened all these years. He could not wait to know his friend again.

Fonzie cut off the winding country road onto a dirt path so narrow Richard did not even see it through the wall of trees until they were already on it. Fonzie lowered his head as far as he could, and Richard did the same, otherwise one of the low-hanging branches reaching out across the path would have hit them. They pulled up to a cabin secluded by trees. There were no neighbors. The bike stopped and the engine cut off. It huffed and then was quiet. It was completely silent except for the engine cooling down and the wind rustling the evergreens. Fonzie got off the bike without a word, looked at Richard through the black visor of his helmet, then headed inside. Richard got off the bike too. He rubbed his arms to bring some warmth back into them.

There was a car parked behind the cabin—Richard could see its tail end sticking out. It was too dark to tell what kind. The windows of the cabin lit up as Fonzie turned on the lights inside. Richard followed him, feeling like he was in a dream.

•   •   •

HE ENTERED THE CABIN. HE WAS STRUCK BY THE *PERMANENCE* OF the place, the solidness of the heavy wood furniture, the large wool rugs. There were built-in bookshelves—Richard noticed lots of Joan Didion, some E. M. Forster, *Bright Lights, Big City*, John Updike's new *Witches of Eastwick*. There was a hi-fi stereo system installed on one of the shelves, with records stored in a space below it. Even the walls felt like they had always been here and would be here for good: they were finished, recently so, judging from the scent of paint, and hung with framed art— motorcycles, mostly, and Edward Hopper–like images of mid-century American scenes: gas stations, diners. The fireplace still had gray, burned-out logs in it.

"Is this where you live?"

Fonzie did not answer. He stood in the middle of the cabin with his helmet on and his back to Richard, who stood just inside the door.

"I *knew* you weren't dead," Richard said. "I just knew it. It all just didn't add up. Losing control and crashing? No way. I never believed it for a second. Not for one second."

Fonzie took off his helmet and Richard stopped talking as Fonzie turned to face him.

"Mrs. *Sealock*?" Richard said.

• • •

DISAPPOINTMENT CRUSHED RICHARD. FONZIE WAS STILL DEAD
after all. It was almost worse than when he had heard the news
the first time.

She yanked a chair out from the table. It screeched across the
stone floor. "Have a seat," she said. He sat. She put the helmet upside down on the small wooden table then filled a glass with water
and put it in front of him. He drank it all at once. She was standing there watching him, pulling the leather gloves off her fingers.
She unzipped the leather jacket, peeled it off, revealing a white
tank top, delicate shoulders. She tossed the jacket over the back of
a chair and jammed the gloves inside the helmet. She went to the
fireplace, put in some fresh logs, some newspaper, started a fire.

"You've stumbled into a real mess, Richie. You have no idea
how big."

Her voice was plain, and worn-out. The last time he had seen
her she had seemed tired, but now her voice was completely
stripped of all its full-throated richness and musicality. All of her
warmth was gone, replaced by focused rage.

She came over again to the table. Behind her the fire grew quickly
into bright, wild orange flames. Her normally perfectly styled hair
was tangled and matted on her head. She wore no makeup. Gone
was the straight posture, the eager graciousness. She was boiling
with resolve. Her eyes were seeing Richard, seeing behind him,
and through him, within him—seeing what she was going to say

to him. She smelled like gasoline and leather and cold air. She went to the record player, squatted before the albums, and began sorting through them. He watched the side of her face. It was hard to believe there had ever been a smile on it. She seemed to be listening to something in her ear, an irritating sound. Her eyes blinked rapidly. She sucked on her lips. She breathed heavily, impatiently, like breathing itself was an unjust obligation. He watched her shoulder blades move beneath the fabric of her shirt, the muscles on the backs of her arms. Who the hell was this woman?

"Mrs. Sealock," Richard said.

"Don't call me that," she said. She chose a record. Put it on the turntable. The pop of the needle, the hiss—then the music. Raw guitar—simple drums—then the voice. It was the early stuff, when he was just a wild, lonesome kid misunderstood by the authorities of the world. She sat down in front of the turntable, her back to Richard.

"This one was his favorite," she said. "He always put this one on. It could drive me crazy—I'd hear it as I walked in the door, I'd hear it from *outside* when I arrived. I'd come in and beg him, Please, enough, can we *please* change it up? He'd look at me, surprised, confused, not even realizing that he played it that often. Yeah, he'd say, sure, whatever you want. I'd put on something else, something I liked—David Bowie, Talking Heads, whatever—but it never felt right. And we'd always end up back at Elvis."

"I'm sorry," Richard said, "who are you talking about? Your husband? This is, what, a vacation place?"

She did not answer. She only inhaled deeply—the bones of her back expanding—then exhaled. It made him very nervous about asking her anything else. Either the questions would break her or make her break him. He said nothing, just waited.

The fire was settling—it let out a loud pop. A spark flew out. She stretched her leg and snuffed it out with her boot. "Have you ever loved someone?" she said softly. He could barely hear her.

"My wife," he said.

"Then you know what it's like. Do you remember the moment you met?"

"I do."

"You remember how you felt?"

"Vividly. Like it just happened."

For a moment a smile appeared on her face. He saw her cheeks move. Almost immediately it vanished. "Describe it," she said.

"Okay," he said, "well, everything in me was *drawn* to her. I had never felt such a thing before, for anyone. Whether there is a hand guiding the universe, I don't know. But when I saw her that day, sitting at the table in the library? Well, I'm telling you, it sure felt like there was."

"Was it something you chose?"

"What do you mean?"

"Could you have turned it off? Said no to it?" She turned a little, to look over her shoulder toward him. "Could you have just walked out of that library that day—you and Fonzie—it was the college one, wasn't it? Where you and he had gone to pick up girls?"

"No, I don't think I could have. And how did you know I was there with him?"

"So you know," she said. "It wasn't your fault. You couldn't have ignored it. You couldn't have turned it away, that feeling, right? That love? When it happened, it wasn't your fault." She turned all the way around, looking at him directly, her eyes narrow and fierce, like he had insulted her. "Right? It wasn't your *fault.*"

"No," he said, feeling like he was off balance, "of course it wasn't. Love is never anyone's fault."

Her eyes grew even more narrow; she was scrutinizing him, looking for signs, something he was not saying. But there was not anything he wasn't saying. "Exactly," she said.

"I'm sorry, what are we talking about? How did you know Fonzie was there when I met my wife?"

"He wasn't just *there*," she said. "Was he? He encouraged you to go talk to her. Otherwise you never would have."

"How do you *know* all this, Mrs. Sealock?"

She did not answer right away. He wondered if she had heard him. Then she put her hands on the floor on either side of her, twisted her body, and climbed to her feet. The firelight on her skin made her look lit from within. "I told you. Don't call me that."

"Okay," he said, putting up his hands. "What do I call you then?"

"Shotz."

"Like the beer? I don't understand."

"You will." She sat in a chair and put her elbows on the table and her fingers to the sides of her head. Closing her eyes, she rubbed her temples. He watched her face. She was scowling—like she was suffering from a horrible headache. With her eyes closed and scowling in torment like that, her face reminded him of a bust of a genius artist—Mozart or somebody. Conducting storms of orchestras in the skull.

She breathed deeply again. "My name is Shotz. My maiden name. My family is the Great Lakes' biggest brewer and has been for a hundred years. The result of that, and the cause of it, is we know our way around the Wisconsin political landscape. To say we have influence isn't enough. We have money. Which means we have power."

"Okay," Richard said. "I think I might see where this is going. You and your husband can use your family's influence to get justice for Fonzie."

"No," she said. "That's not where this is going. Not at all." He tried to think, but he could not. The pipes in his head were dripping—faster now, an uncontrollable stream.

She said, "I used to wonder if Martin knew that. When he started slipping me those cookies in the cafeteria line at Northwestern, I thought, here is someone from the real world. A human. This cute guy flirting with me—he doesn't know or care if my family is influential in local politics in another state—he just wants, you know, what any other nineteen-year-old wants. But, Richard, there is nothing about Martin Sealock that is like any other person. No, that is not what he wanted. It took me a long time to figure it out. Who would have even imagined? I'd mention my family, and he'd look like he couldn't care less. He'd even try to change the subject. It was *boring* to him. Listen, you ever throw all your dreams away in Tokyo?"

"Not that I recall."

"I was there for a Chanel shoot. And I'd just gotten word that I'd been offered the contract to be the face of Yves Saint Laurent's spring collection. My dream job. I was out celebrating with my agent and my friend Laurie, another model, who had just gotten a campaign for this up-and-coming designer. She was young— sixteen. I was older, I was twenty, but I looked out for her, she was like my little sister. My agent got drunk and let it slip to us that Laurie's job? They were going to make her look like Lolita. You know, sex her up. It was disgusting. She was a *kid*. She didn't want to do it. My agent said that was too bad, that she had to. I told him if you make her do this, I'll quit modeling. And I did. I went home that night—straight to the airport from that party, flew all the way from Tokyo to Milwaukee. It worked— I was their star. They backed off Laurie and let her not do the campaign. I was ready to return, but by then I'd been home long enough to realize there were more important things to me than all that. It was like I could see two lives."

"Almost like two lines," Richard said. "The bright one is

the one you're living and the faded is the one you should be. They're parallel. You can see the faded one, and you need to get to it, it kills you that you aren't on it, but you don't know how to get to it."

"*Yes*," she said. She was smiling for the first time that night. "That's exactly *right*. I *knew* you'd understand me. He always told me we would get along. So I tore up the contract. I came home. I had this idea that I could be a normal woman, with a family, and do work that helped people, that did something good for the world. That I could live an honest life. That's all I wanted. I was working at a nonprofit, trying to start over. One day I went for lunch across the street to a sandwich place. Someone tapped me on the shoulder. Martin Sealock. I hadn't seen him since Evanston. He had grown even more handsome. He was in a suit. Fate had put us in the same city again. We had coffee later. He was happy and driven and satisfied in his work—everything I wanted. I braced myself for him to tell me about a fiancé or something, but there was none, not even a girlfriend. It seemed like what you said before, the hand of the universe. I thought that's what it was. It's scary how close the difference can be between everything else and the genuine thing. I only found that later. Once the real thing happens, it is so undeniable you can't believe you ever thought anything else was it. But you just don't know until then."

"You're not in love with Martin Sealock. You're in love with somebody else."

"It was not a coincidence that Martin was in that sandwich shop that day. And it wasn't a coincidence that he was in Milwaukee. It wasn't even a coincidence that I had come through Martin's line at the dining hall. He had put himself in that line, knowing it was the one I always went through. He had put himself in Milwaukee because he knew me well enough to know I would come back. He knew who I was before he knew who I was. Do you understand me? It was all calculated from the time he was eighteen years old. Because of my last name and who my father was. He never loved me. He never even liked me. I found that out after we were married, after his first affair, but I didn't want to believe it. He saw me as something that could get him what he wanted, and he lied about loving me to get it. A man willing to lie about love is a man willing to lie about anything. And willing to *do* anything."

"This is a lot," Richard said. "It's a lot."

"You're telling me." The side of the record had ended long ago. She got up and flipped it, then went to the fire, picked up an iron poker from a nearby wrought iron bucket, and used it. Sparks flew and the flames had a burst of life. She squatted on her heels, watching them. Elvis was singing "Tutti Frutti."

"And what gets us here tonight," she said, "is my message."

"Okay," he said, not understanding.

"*Sit on it.*"

The chair scraped loudly against the floor as he pushed back from the table and stood. "That was *you*." She was still.

Her arms were crossed in front of her. He could not see her face.

"Maybe two years ago," she said, "the Jaguar was in the shop. Martin had always been the one to handle the cars—he'd always joked that if he let me near the engine I would only do more damage. He thinks I'm an idiot—that all women are. The garage called to say the car was ready. I was the only one home. I told them no one would be able to make it there to pick it up until the next day. The mechanic on the phone offered to come deliver it. He had a flatbed truck, it was no problem. Free of charge. Martin had always said this guy was the best, and now I could see what he meant. So he comes. He's out in the driveway, unloading our car from the truck. And what you said before, how you felt seeing your wife the first time—I felt that. That's what I *felt*. I can *still* feel it, just remembering it. But I tried to ignore it. I paid him, thanked him, and said goodbye. He probably thought I was rude, I was so short with him. But if I said too much, if I stood there with him too long . . . My *son* was coming home from school soon. So I was relieved when he left. I went back inside. I had work to do, I had to finalize a quarterly budget. Instead I found myself in the garage, looking through the toolbox. I found a hammer, opened the hood of the Jaguar, and took it to the engine. I yanked out whatever I could tear loose. When I was done, my shoulders burned and the engine was obliterated. I went inside and called the mechanic. 'It seems to be broken again.' Innocent, you know? He came back. This time he was on a motorcycle. He looked at me like he was disappointed in me. Like, I don't know, he expected more from me. He opened the hood and asked me to get him a screwdriver. I found one in the garage and gave it to him. That's all he needed. *Maybe* ten minutes later, he closed the hood and said, Okay. He had me sit behind the wheel and give it a try. It worked perfectly. He got back on his motorcycle and drove off." She took a sharp, sudden breath and shivered. "Martin Sealock has looked at me many times over the years. I used to think he was seeing me. But at that moment I knew he never did. Because he never—not even once—ever looked at me the way that mechanic did that day. Like he could see right inside me. Right into my heart. And the next day I went to his house. The address was on his invoice."

"Where?" said Richard, leaning closer, excited at this chance to start filling in the last years of Fonzie's life. "Where did he live?"

"Right above his shop. There was a little studio apartment up there. He didn't keep a lot in it. A hot plate. Secondhand mismatched furniture. An iron, which I used to tease him about, because he didn't own anything that needed ironing. He'd just say, A man needs an iron. No TV. Some books, mostly in stacks on the floor. The only thing on the wall was a letter, in a frame."

"The one I gave him the day I left," Richard said. A surge of emotion went up his torso.

"No, not that one. It was from his father."

"His father? No. He wanted nothing to do with his father."

"I know that," she said. "And I also know it was because his father walked out when Fonzie was just three years old and spent the rest of his life bumming around on boats as if Fonzie didn't exist. Fonzie went his whole life not knowing who or where his father was, until one night when you two were maybe twenty. There was a knock on the door and it was a sailor who said Fonzie's father had sent him to deliver a letter."

Richard said, "The sailor gave it to Fonzie then left. Fonzie didn't want to open it, but my family and I convinced him to."

Margo said, "The first line of the letter said that it had in fact been his father who had delivered it. He didn't have the guts to tell him. And he knew he wouldn't. That's why he wrote it in a letter then left. Fonzie didn't even get a chance to see his face very well."

"The letter," Richard said, "went on to explain why his father left. It wasn't much of an explanation. All it said was that he was a merchant seaman, that he met Fonzie's mother. When she got pregnant he had thought he could settle down like everybody else, but he couldn't. All he said was, 'It just didn't work out.'"

"All his life Fonzie had thought his own father hated him for some reason," Margo said, "that he had done something wrong just by being born. But that night, you and your family made him see that it wasn't his fault at all, it was his father's fault for failing to live up to his responsibility. The whole thing made Fonzie see that *you* were his real family, not that man."

"That's right," Richard said. "No one else knew that except for us. He never told anyone about that, certainly not any of his girlfriends. That he told you says a lot."

"Fonzie told me how much he regretted not calling you after your father died."

"Why didn't he?"

"It was just too painful for him. And then the longer he waited, the more guilty he felt, until he just couldn't do it. He even began avoiding his cousin Chachi because he couldn't face your sister, Joanie. You were the only one he ever trusted, Richie. The only one he ever let his guard down around, the only one who knew the real him. After you left, he said he had no one like that—until me. For twenty years he was back in that shell you'd drawn him out of. He figured he would probably die that way—safe but alone, having only once really connected with another person, that one time being enough. But then I met him and I drew him back out. I restored him. That's why he loved me—I brought him back to life. I got him interested in his old friends again. Started getting out more. I think he was planning to even start going to Arnold's again. But he never got the chance. What he told you was true, at least I'm sure he meant it at the time, but his father's absence never stopped eating at him. It never stopped. Underneath everything, no matter what it was, temporary happiness or pleasure, whatever, he always felt rejected, unwanted. That's why he was such an outsider, such a loner. He grew comfortable with it, accepted it. But he could never be normal. Or happy. He could never relax. It was like he was marked from birth."

"I left him all alone," Richard said. "Once again, he was all alone, with no family."

She reached out toward him but did not touch him. "No, no. He never blamed you. Please understand that. He never, ever did blame you. He's the one who convinced you to leave in the first place. He wanted you to be out there. He was proud of you. He was so proud of you for what you did. He would have never forgiven you if you had come back."

"Did he ever reconnect with his father?"

"No. He died still never knowing his face."

"Did he have any kids?"

"His only babies were his cars and bikes. He ran his own shop. Making custom hot rods and repairing vintage bikes. He was picky about what he worked on, he wouldn't work on just anything, he only worked on bikes and cars for people who sufficiently appreciated and respected and loved them. He made just enough money to stay open."

"So how do you know all this? What happened when you went out to see him that first time?"

"That first time, not much. Fonzie turned me away. He was gentle about it, of course. He said he appreciated the sentiment, and that he thought I was beautiful and smart, but that one of his rules was that he did not date married women. I started coming around the shop—if there was a ticking noise in the engine, or one tire seemed flatter than the others, or *anything*, no matter how small, I brought it in. All I wanted was to be around him. He let me hang around, watch him work. He showed me around an engine. Soon all I wanted was to be around him *and* be around cars and motorcycles. He helped me discover a passion and talent I never knew I had. We'd take breaks, go to lunch. Talk about bikes and our lives, our dreams. I came to know the real Fonzie, the guy he had shown only to you before: the tough guy with impeccable virtue; the philosopher with the grease-covered hands; the lone wolf whose loyalty to those he considered a friend was unbreakable. Fonzie taught me how to ride a motorcycle. It made me feel more peace and freedom than I ever knew possible. He got my first leather jacket and helmet, he even went to the store with me to help me buy my own custom bike. He urged me to get a Triumph, like his, but I wanted a Harley. Local pride, you know? He teased me about it when I first showed up with it at his shop. He called me a Hells Angel. And I called him a traitor because Triumphs aren't American made; they're British. But I could tell he respected me for standing up to his pressure, for making my own decision. Even if I ripped off the design of his—taking off the front fender, putting in ape hangers, painting the gas tank silver. That day I told him about Tokyo. And what I had given up to protect my friend. He just said I was a hell of a woman. Then he said he loved me very much. And then he kissed me."

"But he had a rule about married women. They were off-limits. What about that?"

"In this case it wasn't up to him. Because he was feeling the same thing I was. He said he was making an exception because he was in love with me. And sometimes love breaks rules. He also said it was the first time he had ever told a woman he loved her."

The record ended. They left it alone, the only sound the embryonic rhythms of the finished record spinning beneath the needle.

She said, "I was the first person since you whom he trusted enough to really let his guard down. I made him happy." She looked around. "This was our place. My husband doesn't know about it. I bought it for us, with my own money, like I did my Harley."

Richard said, "So what happened? How did all hell break loose?"

She said, "The way it always does: by telling the truth. The whole truth."

"What do you mean, you mean you told your husband about Fonzie?"

"No, he never knew about us. It was the other way around: I told *Fonzie* about my *husband*. He knew I was married. He knew the whole situation. But he didn't know the real truth about my husband. No one did. I told him, and it was the worst mistake I ever made in my life."

"What are you talking about?"

"The real truth about Martin Sealock," she said, "is that he negotiated a deal with that company."

"Sackett-Wilhelm? But everyone knows about that."

"No, not that deal. That's not the real deal. I overheard him on the phone. The deal he negotiated—the real one—is that Sackett-Wilhelm would announce they were staying in Milwaukee and would credit Martin for their decision. Meanwhile, their lobbyists would donate five million dollars to the campaign. In return, when Martin is elected—and he will be, for keeping Sackett-Wilhelm here—he will return to them three times their donation in tax credits. And this time next year the company will leave for China after all."

Richard was shaking his head, ill. "I don't believe it. I just don't."

"Whether you believe it or not doesn't matter. Every one of those people who work at that factory will be crushed, their families will be crushed, and none of them have the slightest idea what's coming. And it makes no difference to Martin. He doesn't care. Because he will already have been elected governor."

"And you told Fonzie all this."

"He cared more about protecting the people than getting back at Martin—especially knowing Potsie and Ralph work there. So he came to the house one night and told him he knew about the deal. He did not tell him how he knew—only that he knew. He wanted to protect me."

"Martin doesn't know about what was going on?"

"Egomaniac that he is, the idea that his wife would ever fall in love with someone else, let alone with the mechanic? It's just not within the realm of possibilities."

"What'd Fonzie do?"

"He gave him an ultimatum. Tell the people the truth, or he would. He would take what he knew to the *Milwaukee Journal.* Well, Martin broke down. I was outside the door listening. He cried. He begged Fonzie for mercy. He told him he was right about everything, that he had been desperate because he had been so far behind in the polls and wasn't raising money, he had made a horrible mistake. He agreed to come clean. First thing in the morning, he would call a news conference and tell the people everything. He walked Fonzie to the door. Fonzie told him he would help him however he could. Then he left. Martin called someone on the phone. I couldn't hear who. But on his way home, Fonzie crashed."

Richard put his hands to his head. "Okay," he said. "Hold on. Okay."

"As soon as I heard about it, I knew he'd done it, but I didn't know how. I couldn't investigate it myself without Martin finding out. I didn't know what I was going to do, who I could trust— I was *dead* inside. The love of my life was *dead.* And then you showed up. Fonzie had told me so much about his old friend Richie Cunningham. And here you were. It was like you were an angel. It took everything I had, at the memorial service, to keep myself from telling you everything then and there. I tried to tell you at the house, but I couldn't do it. I didn't have the nerve. And Martin doesn't miss a thing. All I could do was try and direct you to the bike and hope you found a clue."

"I found one all right. How'd you know it was at TJ's?"

"Fonzie mentioned once that he got his parts there, that TJ always had good stuff because the cops let him have unclaimed road wrecks. TJ was the closest thing he had to a friend. I thought someone had to have either cut his brakes or monkeyed with his accelerator, or I didn't know what exactly, but I knew that if I could get you there to take a closer look at the bike, then that would make TJ take a look too, and maybe the two of you would see something the cops hadn't—because either they didn't care or had a reason not to look. It was a long shot, but that's all I had." She continued, "It wasn't until tonight that I realized it was that cop on the bridge."

"You know him?"

"No, I've never seen him before. But I'm not surprised Martin has a cop on his payroll. There's probably more than one. Maybe the whole force."

Richard said, "And there's no evidence of the deal to take to the newspaper? No proof?" She shook her head no. He stood up. He paced.

"Martin needs to pay, Richard," she said. "How do we make him pay?"

The fire was dying down. Richard sat on the sofa. The drip, drip in his head had stopped. The two open pipe ends had been connected. The only question that remained was whether Kirk was in on it. Richard would not have pegged him for a dirty cop—if anything, the problem with Kirk was he had always been too clean, obsessively straight. And when Sealock said he wanted to get rid of him, he sounded like he meant it. He sounded like he had meant everything. Richard felt foolish falling for the act. But he was not the only one. The man was a talented actor. Richard had been around enough to know one of the greats. And he had wanted so badly to believe him. After Gleb and *Space Battles,* he had needed someone who was not his wife or his mother to believe in him. And with Fonzie gone, he needed a friend. Sealock had found the easiest mark in the world.

But Richard could act too. He could lie. He had been lying to himself about *Suttree* for years now. He had been lying to himself about himself. He wasn't who he told himself he was. The Corvette. The suits. The famous friends. The name—*Richard*? He wasn't Richard. He was Richie. He always had been and always would be. He realized that now. He had been running in shame from who he was. Sealock was willing to trample whoever got in his way—but for Richard, it was only himself who got in his own way and so only himself who was trampled. But these last few days, being back where he had come from, being around the old friends, he was no longer ashamed, in fact he was proud. From now on he would be honest about who he was and where he had come from.

But first there was one more lie to tell.

"I have an idea," he said. "But it's better if you don't know about it, or it'll put you in danger. Fonzie wanted to keep you out of this."

She took the car, left the bike. Richard waited until she drove off and he could not hear the car's engine anymore. Then he picked up the phone and called the only people he could trust.

"WHAT ARE YOU DOING OUT HERE?" POTSIE SAID AS RICHARD climbed into the back seat of Ralph's Pontiac. "Reenacting *Deliverance?*"

Richard sat leaning forward between the two front seats and filled them in. He told them about Kirk, and about what Margo Sealock had told him. About Sealock they were heartbroken, shocked, angry—and not entirely credulous.

"You don't believe her, do you?" Ralph said.

"I don't know," Richard said. "I don't know who to believe anymore. I don't know exactly what is going on. All I know is Fonzie was killed, and either Sealock or Lieutenant Kirk is responsible, maybe both. Whoever it was, I'm going to bring them down, and I can't do it alone. I need your help. What do you guys say? Up for one more harebrained youthful misadventure, for old times' sake?"

"Absolutely," Ralph said.

Potsie asked, "What do you need?"

"For one thing, a safe place to crash tonight. Sealock knows I'm staying at the old house. The cops probably have it staked out as we speak."

"You can stay in our guest room," Potsie said.

"Perfect," Richard said. "And, Ralph, we're also going to need that new recording equipment you mentioned the other night at Arnold's."

Ralph had started to put the car into gear but now slid it back into park. "Richard," he said, turning around to face him, growing serious. "I appreciate your wanting to get the band back together, but I don't think now's quite the right time to work on our 'Splish Splash.'"

"Hey, Ralph," Richard said.

"Yeah, Richie?"

"Just drive, you bonehead."

WHEN THEY WERE BACK IN TOWN, HE HAD RALPH PULL THE Pontiac over at a phone booth. He stepped inside the Plexiglas-and-aluminum closet, dropped in a quarter, and dialed Sealock. Potsie and Ralph leaned against the booth's open door to listen.

"Richard," Sealock said pleasantly. "How did it go on the bridge? What'd you find?"

"Quite a lot."

"Yeah? Like what?"

"Well, for one thing: a goon. *Your* goon."

"Yes—Sauer. He told me." His voice was warm and friendly as always.

"Good," Richard said, "then he also told you that Fonzie's still alive. That was him on the bike. You thought you could kill him? You thought you could kill *Fonzie*? You're not man enough. You're not even halfway there. He survived your lousy hit job, he was alive when he hit the water and swam away. Didn't anyone teach your muscleman to shoot a few holes in them to make sure the job was done right?"

Potsie and Ralph were guffawing at Richard's performance. He waved his hand at them and put a finger to his lips to shush them.

"If that's your best Philip Marlowe," Sealock said, "it's more Elliott Gould than Humphrey Bogart. Who's that with you?"

"Who do you think? It's Fonzie. Now listen up. We want to make a deal. Give me the money I need to make my movie."

Sealock scoffed. "That's a lot of money."

"A *lot* of money. Five million dollars. The exact amount you got from Sackett-Wilhelm."

"That money's spent, Richard."

"What's left of it?"

"A million. At most."

"That'll have to do then."

"And what is that buying me?"

"My silence."

"And the greaseball?" said Sealock. "How much does Fonzie want?"

"He doesn't want your money. All he wants is to get far away from this lousy place and start a new life somewhere else. You beat him, okay? You won."

"It's going to take time to get that money together," Sealock told him. "It's not liquid. It's tied up in various accounts and holdings."

"Out in Hollywood, we have a saying," Richard said. The words just came out, he said them before he had thought it through, there wasn't really any saying he had in mind, and now his brain scrambled for something. All he came up with was: "You've got until tomorrow night."

"It's not a very exciting saying," Sealock said.

"Tomorrow night. Seven o'clock. Meet me at the Cheesehead Lodge on South Kinnickinnic. You know it?"

"I know it."

"And if you're getting your hopes up about getting another shot at Fonzie or any other kind of monkey business, know this: I'll be alone. Fonzie won't be there. If I don't meet him with the money at ten o'clock tomorrow night, he's going straight to the papers. Like he should have done in the first place."

He hung up. He let out a deep breath and fell atop the phone, his forehead on his arm. Then he lifted his head and turned to Potsie and Ralph and held out his hands. They were shaking.

POTSIE SCOOPED OUT TWO DISHES OF HAMBURGER HELPER from the pan his wife had left on the stove. She and the girls were already in bed when he and Richard arrived. "Voilà," he said, presenting a plate to Richard, who was sitting at the kitchen table. "The San Francisco treat."

"I think you're thinking of Rice-A-Roni, Potsie."

Potsie shrugged. He opened a Shotz for himself and poured milk into a glass for Richard. They ate. Richard was starved—the day and all its tortured anxiety had scooped him out. He ate with the ferocity of an animal. Eating had always made him think. Sometimes he could almost feel his brain releasing the thoughts as he ate, like they were something physical, like a flock of small colorful birds. This time every single one of his thoughts involved one of three people: Caroline. Richie Jr. Lori Beth.

Potsie must have been thinking along the same lines because he said, with his mouth full, "What would you say is the worst part of being a parent?"

"Easy," Richard said, his mouth full too. He swallowed. "The constant terror."

"Yeah, I know what you mean. Can you imagine how it gets around here in the mornings with two teenage girls? We have only three bathrooms. It's not enough. Three bathrooms. I've got to think about putting in a *fourth*."

"No, I mean being afraid *for* them all the time."

"Oh yeah."

"That's the worst part. That constant, low-grade buzz in the back of your head that something terrible will happen to them. The word *anxiety* doesn't begin to cover it. No one really talks about that part of it. They talk about the responsibility, maybe the stress. Never the terror."

"Yeah, no kidding," said Potsie. "And it never goes away."

"Never."

"When Kelly was first born, I held her so gently, I was worried about breaking her. Then I always overdressed her because I was terrified of letting her be cold. I thought it would go away and I'd relax. But I did the same thing with Sarah. And now I still do it, even though it's just other things. Like the way I talk to them. Always afraid of breaking them. But then again, you know, that's the best part too."

"What do you mean?"

"Having that feeling is awful. But it's also kind of beautiful. To care about another person so deeply, so intensely—you can only feel like that when it's your kid, when you're responsible for their life. When everything—your sanity, your *heart, everything*—is at risk just by loving them."

"You think we're as good as our parents? I mean, you think we've done as well? As dads? As guys?"

"Geez, Cunningham." Potsie shook his head, sipped his beer. "We're doing okay."

"We could do better. *I* could, anyway."

"We're doing okay," Potsie repeated. "Our parents were a tough act to follow. Look, what was their big cause when they were young? Hitler. They had Hitler. There's nothing confusing about Hitler—he's evil, you go over, you fight him. Simple, right? Meanwhile, what did we have?"

"Vietnam."

"I mean, are you kidding me? *Vietnam?* The most confusing foreign policy thing in the history of our country? And we're supposed to understand it at such a young age? We're supposed to know if it's something we should kill or die for?"

"Yeah," Richard said, done with his food, folding his arms on the table before him and staring down at his plate, thinking.

"And then what?" continued Potsie. "The postwar years. Booming economy, all that. You got a job, your company loved you, you stayed there for the rest of your life, you had enough for a good life for your family. Again: simple. It was easy to hold on to their values and to see right from wrong, to know which way was forward, which way was backward. And what did we get? Recession. *Assassinations.* Nixon. We got a whole other kind of world. Yeah, our parents were great. But I would have liked to see them with *our* wars, and *our world.* See what kind of time they would have had sorting it all out. I think they would agree with me when I say that we've done a pretty good job. We've turned out very well. I think they'd be very happy. And *proud.*"

"Hey, Potsie, look, you don't have to come tomorrow. You and Ralph, you shouldn't be there. I can set up the microphone and the tape recorder myself. You don't need to be involved. You should be home with your families."

"What are you talking about?"

"I don't want anything to happen to you guys."

"Nothing's going to happen. It'll be fine." From the tone of his voice, Richard could tell Potsie himself was not so sure. "We're going to be there tomorrow night, and that's all there is to it."

They finished their drinks, then Richard tried to do the dishes, but Potsie would not let him. He scrubbed a plate with a sponge. "So ol' Fonzie fell in love," he said thoughtfully, almost singing it. "I have to say, there are worse ways to go out."

Richard had to admit he had a point. The Fonz's ending was not such a tragic one.

Potsie shut off the water and dried his hands. "I gotta hit the hay. You should too. Big day tomorrow. We have to take down the governor."

"He's not the governor yet."

"Not if we can help it, no."

Potsie lurched up the stairs and down the hall, Richard following. Potsie gestured with his head at the guest room. Richard stopped there. "'Night, Potsie." He watched as Potsie stopped before Kelly's closed bedroom door and listened, seemed satisfied by what he heard, then stopped at Sarah's door and did the same. Silence in both rooms. Richard knew what Potsie felt: there is no peace like knowing your children sleep tight.

• • •

RICHARD WENT INTO THE GUEST ROOM AND SAT ON THE BED. HE
stared into the darkness. He listened to himself breathe, felt his
heart beating in his chest. Then he stood up again and went back
downstairs. He picked up the phone and called to cancel his
flight. Then he rang Lori Beth.

"The edit is running long," he told her. "It's going to be one
more day. Maybe more."

As usual, she could tell something was wrong.

"Richard."

"You know, it's what happens. It's not right yet. We have to
make it right. I love you. And Richie Jr. And Caroline. I love
you all very much. Very much." Then he said, "Good night, Lori
Beth."

He did not know if it would be the last time he ever spoke
to her.

HE COULD NOT SLEEP. HE KEPT JOLTING UPRIGHT WITH EVERY CAR
that passed by on the otherwise silent, tree-lined street, thinking
it was Officer Sauer, that he had found him here. Officer Sauer
or Lieutenant Kirk—who for all Richard knew was still involved
in all this. He worried about putting Potsie and his family in
danger by hiding out here. What a good guy Potsie was. One of
the best people he had ever known. He and Ralph both. That had

always been true, but maybe he had forgotten it—it was certainly highlighted now, after all this. There are no friends like the kind you make when you're young. It is like you meet the earth's best people before you turn eighteen, and then after that it's just a matter of learning the true depth of their goodness, and being continually astounded by it, by how there is no bottom to it, the goodness just goes and goes.

His body was antsy with the urge to leave—take off, get a cab, go to the airport, fly home—but he did not act on it, he just lay there, his mind spinning, not knowing what to do or what to think, wondering if he was making a mistake and if so how serious it was, and how grave its consequences would be. He thought of Fonzie and how much he wished the story he had fed Sealock tonight was true—he wished that Fonzie was still alive. Being friends again with Ralph and Potsie was great, but he wished he could be friends again with Fonzie too. If he had that, he would have it all. God, how he wished Fonzie was alive. He might have even made the wish out loud. You might have called it a prayer.

FRIDAY

THE CHEESEHEAD LODGE HAD SEEN BETTER DAYS. MOST OF them were right around the first Super Bowl.

In the parking lot the orange sodium lights were on. Night had fallen. They found their rooms—room 15 and room 66, which were next door to each other, connected by a door. The rooms at the Cheesehead Lodge, which was laid out like a motel, were numbered after the jersey numbers of famous Green Bay Packers players. The office had rented them Bart Starr and Ray Nitschke.

They opened the door to Bart Starr. They smelled the room before they saw it—a moldy musk hit them like a bear hug. Richard flipped on the light, revealing walls covered in wood paneling on which hung portraits, action photos, oil paintings, and framed, signed jerseys of the legendary quarterback. The closet was made to look like a locker, nameplate included. The carpet was Packer yellow. The archaic television was Packer green. The lamps in the corner and on the bedside tables had Packer helmets for a base, wedges of cheese for the shade. Packer ashtrays sat overflowing with cold, smoked butts.

"Hey," Ralph said, carrying a box of recording equipment, "this place is nice."

He went through the connecting door to Ray Nitschke and began setting up the microphone and tape recorder. A taped confession was their only hope for proving Sealock had Fonzie murdered. Richard would meet with him in Bart Starr while Potsie and Ralph hid in Ray Nitschke, secretly recording the conversation through the wall. Richard watched Ralph. He examined the microphone. "Are you sure this thing is strong enough to work?"

"That's a Neumann," Ralph told him. "Top of the line. That thing's so sensitive it could make a mouse's fart sound like a cymbal crash."

Richard knocked on the wall between the two rooms. "About as thin as they get. Just don't sneeze or anything. He'll hear you."

"What do you think we are, idiots?" Ralph was trying to untangle a cord.

Potsie was looking through the blinds out at the parking lot. He turned around. "Man, this is cool. It's just like *Miami Vice*."

"It's on tonight," Ralph said. "Think we'll be done in time to watch it?"

Potsie said, "We better be. You know, people tell me I remind them of Crockett."

"No way," Ralph said. "If anyone's Crockett, it's me."

Potsie said, "*I'm* Crockett. *You're* Tubbs."

"You're Crockett's pet alligator."

"No way are you Crockett. You're not cool enough to be Crockett. Richard, tell Potsie he's not cool enough to be Crockett."

Potsie said, "*He* doesn't care about *Miami Vice,* he probably watches *Falcon Crest.*"

"Enough goofing around," Richard said, "we've only got a few minutes."

Ralph set the mixer and tape recorder on the table—crusted with old spilled beer—and sat down in one of the chairs, slipped on the headphones, and hit the switch on the tape recorder. "Okay," he said to Potsie, giving him a thumbs-up, "let's check the levels."

Potsie nodded, a competent assistant. He leaned down into the microphone and shouted into it, "TESTING TESTING!"

Ralph winced, tore off the headphones. "Ah!" he said. He stuck a finger in his ear.

"Sorry," Potsie said. "Hey Richard, let's test it out." Richard went next door and spoke while Potsie and Ralph recorded through the wall. "Hello, hello," he said. He returned and they played it back. He listened through the headphones—his voice was clear.

"Okay," Richard said. "Are we ready?"

Potsie said, "Ready, Richard."

"Ralph? We ready?" He did not answer. "Ralph." Ralph looked up, like he had been daydreaming. "We ready?"

He gave Richard a thumbs-up. "Yeah, Richard." He stuck a finger in his ear again, opened and closed his mouth, like his jaw hurt.

"Okay. Good luck. And, guys. One last thing."

"What's that?" Potsie said.

"From now on? I'm Richie."

There was a knock on the front door of the other room.

IN HIS OFFICE AT HIS HOUSE JUST YESTERDAY, SEALOCK HAD been an entirely different person, so kind and warmhearted and *good*, but this man standing here outside the open door of the motel room was all menace and viciousness. Richie had the feeling this was not Sealock but a body snatcher, though he knew it was the other way around: *this* was the real guy and it was the other who had been the fake. Sealock was looking at him sideways, his head turned slightly, his chin tucked into his chest, sick pallor to his skin. "You carrying?" he said to Richie in a tight voice filled with phlegm.

"No," Richie said without thinking it over, then thought better of it and changed his answer. "I mean, yeah, maybe, I might be. What about you?"

"I wouldn't tell you if I was." Sealock stepped inside, shoving past Richie.

"Neither would I," Richie said lamely. "Where is it?"

Sealock reached inside his coat and pulled out an envelope. He handed it to Richie. Inside was a check for a million dollars, from a corporation Richie had never heard of with an address in the Cayman Islands.

Sealock looked around at the room. "I hate the Packers. Football, hunting—that's all anyone in this state cares about. It's depressing." Then he turned to Richie and said, "Okay, hands up."

Richie hesitated.

Sealock was impatient. "I have to search you for a wire," he explained. "Come on, shirt up."

Richie felt smart because he knew Sealock would not find one. Yes, he had been real smart. He was proud of himself for thinking everything through. He lifted the tail of his shirt and turned in a circle. Sealock stayed across the room, keeping his distance, watching with evident distaste. Compared to what Sealock was wearing—a fancy double-breasted suit that was probably Belvest, shiny expensive-looking black wingtips that were probably Hugo Boss—Richie felt like he was dressed very poorly in flannel and denim. It was this new way Sealock was looking at him—like he was nothing, like he was scum. No longer a hotshot who could do something for him. Just another loser. This was the true way Sealock saw Milwaukeeans, Richie realized.

Sealock was satisfied he was not being recorded. He stepped

back and told Richie, "Cover yourself. And consider doing a sit-up now and again. You have no definition in your abs. No wonder you're failing, Richard: you look like garbage."

"Why'd you do it?" Richie said, trying to get him talking. "Why'd you make that deal with Sackett-Wilhelm? How could you have done that to all those people?"

"What did I do? I didn't take away their jobs. That decision was *made*. All I did was give them another year of work, of security. If not for me, they all would be on the street right now. Because of me, their families are fed, and they don't have to worry. Fonzie wanted to take that away from them. So who's the bad guy and who's the good one here, Richard?"

"You're so twisted you can't even see the difference anymore."

"No, I can see it. He had principles, right? Morals?"

"Exactly."

Sealock smiled at him. "Sure." Then he turned his head toward the door and called out, "Okay, Officer."

The door opened. In stepped Officer Sauer, who had been waiting right outside.

He was in uniform and had Margo—his forearm across her throat, a gun to her head. She was gagged with a bandanna. Her eyes were big and white with rage and terror. They fell on Richie but did not seem to see him. Margo fought in his grip, squealing through the gag, but the cop easily restrained her. Her hands were cuffed behind her back. In Sauer's hand not holding the gun was clutched a small black bag that looked like a shaving kit.

"What is this?" Richie said. His eyes darted to the wall behind which were Potsie and Ralph.

"Some moral code," Sealock said.

Sauer put down the satchel and shoved Margo onto the bed. Sealock and Sauer did not give Richie an explanation. She was still looking that way at Richie but now tears were falling down her cheeks. The way Sauer was handling her was how a farmer handles a lamb on the way to the chopping block.

Richie scrambled to regain control. "What's going on?" It was desperate, hopeless. Sealock shushed him like he was an annoying child. He shushed Margo too. Sauer was uncuffing one of her hands in order to chain her to the headboard. He tried to hold the free hand down, but she got it loose and punched him in the mouth. He cursed and spit blood. Sealock was laughing at him. Sauer cursed again, wiped his mouth with his hand, then got her hand secured. Her arms were splayed wide against the headboard. She struggled, but it was no use. She turned her head and faced a mirror on the wall. Once she saw herself, she calmed down, went still and silent, except for a sad little moan, like her reflection was somebody else, another person, a child on TV.

"I give her credit," Sealock said. "She was smart. I never had a clue. She hid it well. Luckily, the city of Milwaukee has well-trained law-enforcement officers, because last night on the bridge Officer Sauer here caught the motorcycle's plate. Didn't think that through, did you?" he said to Margo. "He ran it, found it was registered to Fonzie. For a while there, we actually thought

Fonzie really *was* alive, that we *had* failed to kill him. I had that check issued and was really going to give it to you tonight."

It was all Richie could do to keep his eyeballs from looking to the wall, behind which was the microphone recording what Sealock had just confessed to. *We got him. Run. Take it to the paper. Send their reporters down here. Don't call the cops—they're in on it. Go. Run. Already be gone.*

"But then Sauer, thorough as he is, traced the motorcycle's title back to the Harley dealership that sold it. The owner had a pretty interesting story. He said he didn't sell any Harley to Fonzie—Fonzie was a Triumph man, everyone knew that—but he'd sold one to the girl Fonzie was with. Fonzie was just there to help her pick it out. Guy said he remembered she was a gorgeous woman. Tall. She had short dark hair, like what's her name— 'Love Is a Battlefield.' She wore big sunglasses even inside, like she did not want to be recognized. Guy said he figured she must be somebody famous who didn't want to be bothered. An actress, maybe." He turned to Margo—looked at her in pure disgust. "Or a model."

Her eyes were closed. Tears were still falling down the side of her face into her ears. Her chest was heaving.

"Do you know," Sealock said, his voice rising, "do you have any *clue* what would have happened if the voters of Wisconsin had found out you were screwing around on me? And with some *mechanic*? Some *nobody*? They'd have all thought I was *weak. Weak.* No one likes a weakling—and no one sure as hell *votes* for one."

Sauer had another set of cuffs. He handed his gun to Sealock, who pointed it at Richie. "No, no," Richie said. Then Sauer was wrestling him to the bed beside Margo, cuffing him just like she was.

"However," Sealock said, tapping his finger thoughtfully on his lips. "My wife cheating on me with some slick Hollywood hotshot? One of those West Coast creeps with no respect for traditional family values? The great Richard Cunningham comes back to the town he left in the dust and seduces former model Margo Sealock, who everyone knows secretly deep down always thought she was too good for Milwaukee. She couldn't resist. They shacked up at this motel. Her moral weakness extended beyond mere adultery—she was also a drug fiend."

Sauer went to the small satchel he had brought in. He unzipped it, opened it. The heroin and syringe inside still had the labels from the Milwaukee Police Department evidence room. There was a Bic disposable lighter in there, a spoon, a cotton ball. Sauer went to the table, sat down, and began cooking up two massive shots.

"Twelve pounds they pulled in at that bust the other day," said Sealock. "They won't miss a few grams."

Sauer placed the needle in the liquid and drew back the plunger, filling the syringe.

Sealock said, "But oh no." His face took on an unconvincing frown. "They do too much. It's a shame. And, unfortunately, an all-too-common occurrence in society today. They should have listened to the first lady, Nancy Reagan: Just Say No. Guess they didn't know their own limits. Just like Fonzie riding too fast on a wet road. That poor Martin Sealock. That poor boy of his. Sealock knows firsthand the dangers of drugs. If anyone can fix it, he can. I gotta thank you, Richard. This will work way better than your commercial. And speaking of . . ." He glanced at the clock, then turned on the TV. "I think it should be airing soon."

Through the wall came a very loud voice from the next room. "HEY, POTSIE, THIS IS BAD, I THINK WE SHOULD CALL 911." Then, "WHAT'D YOU *HIT* ME FOR? I *AM* WHISPERING."

Richie's blood became cold and thick.

Sauer froze and looked up at Sealock, who was turning with a very surprised but also very pleased expression on his face toward the source of the voice. "Ah," Sealock said, delighted. He walked up to the wall, extended one finger, and pinned it there—*thump*. "Gotcha," he whispered. He looked at Richie with a grin, then nodded his head at Sauer. He did not have to; Sauer was already taking the gun back from him and going to the door connecting the two rooms. He vanished into it and returned holding Potsie and Ralph both by the collars of their shirts.

"Well hello," Sealock said to them, like they had come by to visit.

"Sorry, Richie," Potsie said.

"No," Richie said, "I am."

Sauer stuffed towels into Potsie's and Ralph's mouths and

used the cords from the recording equipment to tie their hands and their belts to bind their ankles then lay them on the floor like two rolls of carpet. Then he stood up and went back into the Ray Nitschke room. He returned with the tape of the confession Sealock had just inadvertently recorded. The tape they needed to put him away. He handed it to Sealock, who looked it over then ripped out all its ribbon and tore it, destroying it.

Gone.

He and Sauer looked down at Potsie and Ralph.

"What do you want to do with them?" said Sauer.

Sealock shrugged. "Kill them."

"I only have enough for two."

"Then take them out somewhere and put a bullet in their heads. But first finish *them* off," he said, indicating Richie and Margo. "And make it fast—I have a speech at the teachers' union in an hour." He hummed "Boys of Summer" as he turned away, sat on the edge of the bed at Richie's and Margo's feet, and watched the television. It was nearly eight—Richie's commercial was set to air in just a few minutes.

Sauer was approaching Richie with the syringe, loaded up with the hot shot.

Richie could only think of Caroline and Richie Jr. and Lori Beth. Marion too. What would they think if he was found dead in bed with another woman? It would look just as bad as Sealock wanted. Nobody alive to tell them the truth. They would all have to carry that with them the rest of their lives—the idea that they had not really known him at all, that he had been just as much a fraud as Sealock really was.

"Don't do this, Martin," he said.

"Shut up." Then he said to Sauer, "Shut him up."

Sauer snatched the pillow from under Richie's head. He took off the pillowcase and shoved it into Richie's mouth. Richie choked. His eyes watered.

"We should strip them," Sauer said.

"Why?" said Sealock.

"It would lend credibility."

"Do it after," said Sealock.

Richie could hear the faint rolling sounds of thunder outside. A storm beginning. Sauer was taking Richie's forearm, twisting it to reveal the fleshy white underside. The needle was dripping. Sauer was cold, inhuman as he lowered it to Richie's skin. Once the needle pricked through and the plunger went down, death would be almost instant. Richie squirmed and screamed into the pillowcase but it was all useless, there was nothing to be done.

The storm outside was coming on very quickly—the thunder was booming. Irritated, Sealock turned the TV up louder and leaned closer to it. He did not want to miss even one second of his own performance when the commercial aired.

Sauer stopped, looked up. "What is that?" he said. "Lightning?"

There was a light coming in through the window in the

wall by the door—a very bright light that was growing steadily brighter as the thunder grew louder, more intense.

Sauer and Sealock looked at each other.

Sealock said, "Check it out."

Sauer put down the needle, giving Richie a few blessed moments more of life. He spent them trying uselessly to break free.

Sauer went to the front door, opened it. The light burst into the room. It was blinding. Everyone turned their heads from the door. The noise was deafening. And it was not thunder.

Sauer looked back at Sealock. He was scared.

Sauer raised his gun with one hand, used his other hand to shade his eyes. He went through the door and disappeared into the light. It seemed to consume him. The roar cut off. Richie heard Sauer scream. Then a single gunshot. Then there was silence. Nothing but the light.

Sealock sat on the edge of the bed, frozen, watching the door. "Sauer?" he said, hesitant. His voice was suddenly very small. "What do I do?" he whispered to himself. "What do I do?"

Richie's eyes had adjusted to the light. He could look into it. A figure appeared. The rays of light hit it and shattered on all sides of it. It began moving toward them. It was a person. A single, solitary figure. Richie could not see who it was. The figure walked slowly, staggering toward the room, growing larger and larger with every step.

The figure's silhouette was unmistakable.

But it made no sense.

Richie's heart knew better than his mind. It was leaping already before he could understand what he was seeing.

Because the figure emerged, stepping out of the shadows, and they all saw who it was.

The jacket—perfect.

The jeans—perfect.

The hair—perfect.

Maybe he was a little grayed and maybe he walked with a limp, his face grimacing with every step; maybe he wasn't as thin as he had been as a kid, and maybe his eyes had heavy dark circles under them now and there were cuts on his bearded face—but none of it mattered—he was still how Richie remembered him.

Just like how we *all* remembered him.

He stepped into the room. He was wincing in pain and clutching his ribs. He took a slow look around. His gaze stopped on Richie. He leaned back. He stuck out his arms, raised his thumbs.

"Ay," he said.

SEALOCK STOOD. "IT'S IMPOSSIBLE."

That's exactly what it was, Richie was thinking—a miracle. He was laughing through the fabric in his mouth. Eyes shut, whole body shaking with relieved delirium.

Fonzie reached behind himself, into his waistband. He

pointed Sauer's gun at Sealock. He stuck his other hand out and lowered it, and Sealock sat back down. "Park it," Fonzie said. "I got something to show you." Keeping the gun on Sealock, he straightened his jacket then went to the bed, to Margo and Richie. He was trying to hide his limp.

He pulled the bandanna out of Margo's mouth. She was sobbing, laughing through her tears.

He put his hands on the sides of her face and said, "I didn't know. I didn't know they had you." He kissed her. "I would have come right away." He had the keys to her cuffs—he had taken them off Sauer.

"I know."

"I would have kicked down the door, I would have never let him touch you. You know that, right? You know that?"

"I know it, Arthur. I know."

He got her cuffs off, and she put her hands on both sides of his head and kissed him, locked her hands behind his neck, and held him there. Sealock made a noise like a trapped animal. Fonzie opened his eyes and looked at him, but Sealock, eyeing the gun, stayed where he was. Fonzie looked at Richie. Margo let him go. He reached over, plucked the pillowcase out of Richie's mouth. "Hiya, Red. Nice bracelets. Wanna take them off?" As he moved around the bed to free Richie, he saw Potsie and Ralph on the floor. "What are you two doing down there?" He bent down, took the towels out of their mouths. "You better stay put. Keep you from bungling this any further."

"I don't believe this," Sealock said. "You're supposed to be dead."

Fonzie shrugged. "And you're supposed to be a good guy." Sealock was standing up again. Fonzie said, raising his voice, "Where do you think you're going? I said park it." Sealock sat. "It's storytime. You don't want to miss storytime, do you?"

Sealock said nothing. He remained sitting in silence.

Fonzie said, "It was a dark stormy night. Well, maybe not so much stormy as *misty*, but you get the picture. There I was, riding along on the bridge, minding my own business. Out of nowhere some cop comes up and starts hassling me. No big deal—nothing I ain't used to. But this time was different. This one didn't just want to tease me for having a little personality, or bust me for having a mind of my own, oh, no no—this cop wanted to take me out. I knew exactly who was behind it: the creep screwing over my old friends, the jerk bringing pain to the finest woman I've ever known. She brought me back to the land of the living and now said creep was trying to knock me back out of it. This cop gives me a bump, I go skidding, I could have recovered, maybe, but it would only delay the inevitable. So I let myself hit the guardrail." He put his hands over his chest. "It broke my heart seeing my bike go through that. I flew over the handlebars, and made like Greg Louganis. I hit the water perfect. Nary a splash. We're talking gold medal all the way—unless the Soviet judge screwed me. I let the current take me down the shore a few miles. When I finally got out of the water, I had some minor boo-boos, but nothing a little dab of motor oil here and there couldn't fix. Then I got straight to work."

Sealock was shaking his head and saying calmly, "It's unbelievable."

Richie said, "How'd you know where to find us tonight?"

"Mary at the front desk. She's an old girlfriend. She tipped me off. All my old girlfriends have been hiding me, protecting me, keeping me and my secret safe. That's something you never learned, Sealock. You treat people right, they treat you right in return."

Margo said, "You said you got to work—got to work how?"

"Avenging my own death. And building my case against this bucket of slime, to make sure he'd never so much as get a *look* at the governor's mansion."

"It's unbelievable," Sealock said again. His voice was almost taunting.

"I *know* it is," Fonzie said. "People had hope in you."

"No—what you're saying, it's *not believable*. Whatever you plan to say, whoever you plan to tell, who do you think is going to believe you? You have no confession. You have no evidence at all. It's your word against mine. You're nothing. An overgrown juvenile delinquent stuck in his glory days. But me? I've got connections in this town."

Fonzie shrugged and pulled something out of the inside pocket of his jacket. A bundle of documents, folded in half. "Yeah, you've got your connections," he said, "and I've got mine."

He peeled one of the documents off the stack and threw it at Sealock. "Like Sheila at First Wisconsin Bank." He threw another document. "And Monica at *Second* Wisconsin Bank." He threw another. "Michelle at Wisconsin Telephone." He held the last in the air a moment. "Then there's Ruth at Sackett-Wilhelm. She was especially helpful. A real sweetheart." He threw the final document at Sealock, who had not moved, did not even look at the paper.

Richie was going around picking them up off the floor. "It's all here," he said, sorting through them. "Bank activity. Phone records. Handwritten notes. Office visitor logs. It's everything we need."

There came a flurry of sirens outside, far away. They were screaming. Several Milwaukee Police Department cars arrived, jumping the curb into the motel parking lot.

"We have to get out of here," Richie said. "We don't know who else Sealock is working with. The cops are *in* on it! Go!"

"Where is he?" Lieutenant Kirk said, his voice a chilling bark as he entered the room. "Where's Fonzarelli?" He had his gun drawn. They all put their hands up. Fonzie had put Sauer's gun on the ground. With Kirk were half a dozen cops. Outside it looked like the entire force was arriving.

Richie said, "Careful, Fonzie, he's in on it."

Kirk said, "In on what?"

"Fonzie's murder."

"How could I have murdered him? He's standing right here."

"*Attempted* murder then."

Kirk said, "Son, listen to me and listen closely. I have no pleasures in life but one: arresting, hounding, and otherwise harassing Arthur Fonzarelli. Without him around, I wouldn't have any pastimes. I'd have to take up stamp collecting. Who wants to do that?"

Fonzie said, "He's right, Richie. He's clear. He's here because I called him."

Kirk said, "Fonzarelli."

"Yeah?"

"You have to understand—"

"Sure."

"There was so much."

"I know."

"The governor, the city—this place isn't what it used to be."

"You're telling me."

"I'm trying to apologize."

"Forget about it."

"I blew it on this one. I wasn't as good as I should have been. There's no excuse. I'm sorry."

One of the other cops shouted, "Drop it!"

They all turned to him, then to who he was shouting at. In the commotion in that little crowded room, they had all almost forgotten about Sealock. In one hand he held the syringe containing the hot shot that Sauer had been ready to inject into Richie's bloodstream. His other arm was extended, its sleeve up. He held the syringe with the needle pointed downward, right up against his skin, ready to plunge its contents into himself.

"No, no, no," Fonzie said quietly, reaching toward him.

Sealock put his thumb on the plunger. Margo cried out.

Before he could do himself in, something on the TV caught his eye, made him stop.

It was a massive empty space—gray, concrete. There was little light. It took a moment to realize there was somebody in that airplane hangar–size room. This man was at the far end of it, heading toward the camera. As he grew closer you started to make out his gray suit, his blue tie. The machinery had been turned off. He was alone. He walked straight ahead, in a perfect line. His strong jaw was set. His eyes were steady, but kind. He was undaunted by the magnitude of the space, the dormant might of the equipment. His wooden soles clapped on the bare stone floor, and that was all you heard.

Then from either side of him, coming from outside the frame, appeared people. They were workers, swarming in, falling in behind him, smiles on their faces, pride. There were a thousand of them. And they kept coming. A multitude of workers that just never stopped. Their safety goggles around their necks, their gloves in their hands. They were all in blue jumpsuits. On the right side of their chest, their name. On the other side, over their heart, their company's: Sackett-Wilhelm.

The camera remained still. The workers and this man they followed were walking toward it, a procession of cheerful steadfastness.

They were secure, behind their leader. Their savior. And all you heard were the footsteps. The steady, unstoppable walking of people marching forward—toward greater things, better days.

They kept coming. It was like they were going to walk right over the camera, trampling it and anything else in their way. Just as the frame would have cut off his head, the leader stopped. The workers stopped with him. Now there was nothing but silence. The leader looked into the camera. He was on the screen and in the room. There were two of them, and they were impossible to reconcile. On the screen Sealock's eyes twinkled as he looked into the camera, into the room, and said his line:

"Don't just take it from *me*."

A sudden cut to a new camera angle, from high above, showing the entire mass of the gathered workers. It filled the factory. It could have been the crowd at a rock concert. All at once they cried out, "Vote Sealock!" and cheered, waving their hands and arms, ecstatic. And then, also all at once, every machine in that place turned on, roared to life.

The screen went black.

In the room, Sealock dropped the needle. He was shaking his head in admiration and looking at Richie with a big smile. He rose to his feet, clapping. They all watched him. What finally stopped his clapping was Kirk taking his hands by the wrists, twisting them behind his back, and cuffing them. Kirk led him out of the room and put him in the back of a squad car and took him to jail, discarding the wreckage that used to be a hero.

THE WEEKEND COMES

B ENNIGAN'S WAS DEAD. THE STAFF LINED UP AT THE windows, looking out longingly across the street at the party that had killed it. The only cars in its lot were those that couldn't find spots at Arnold's Drive-In. No one was chasing them out. All any of the waiters and bartenders cared about tonight was the clock running out on their shifts so they could rip off their green shirts and go join the party.

The Arnold's parking lot had not been this crowded since the days when it had been filled with carhops. Even the turnout at Fonzie's funeral was nothing compared to this. Lieutenant Kirk and his police officers were there directing traffic, politely guiding cars to empty spots. There was not a ticket book to be seen—all parking rules were suspended for the evening, at the behest of the guest of honor. Kirk was happy to oblige him.

From the open window of an arriving car blasted Frank Stallone's "Far from Over." In the long, disorderly line clamoring to get inside, a woman who was three-fourths Aqua Net and one-fourth leopard print spandex yelled out, "Far from over is right!" A cheer went up through the crowd.

Because last night, mere days after they thought he was dead, the Lord of Cool had risen again and proven himself immortal.

Some come back for Easter Sunday, others come back for Saturday night.

INSIDE, THE BAND ON THE RISER, MEN WHO WORK, WAS IN THE second verse of "Separate Ways" by Journey. Potsie Weber on vocals. Ralph Malph on bass. Each member wore a similar Springsteen-esque ensemble of a flannel shirt with sleeves cut off, and torn blue jeans, and a bandanna around his head. Above the drummer, a Sackett-Wilhelm second-shift assembler, was a banner proclaiming:

FONZIE LIVES!

THE DANCE FLOOR WAS BEYOND CAPACITY, THE AIR DANK WITH sweat. Margo and Fonzie stood at the outer edges, Fonzie's arm around his woman, taking in the scene. He was cleaned up and wearing his leather jacket—the only person who could even think about wearing a coat in that steaming hot room—and even so he still had not broken a sweat, not a single strand of his salt-and-pepper hair out of place.

Al snaked through the crowd, emerging from between two gyrating women with his face glowing red from the heat and the exhilaration, delivering plates to a table. He dropped them off, then came over and threw his arms around Fonzie, kissed his cheek.

"How you doing, Al?" said Fonzie.

"How am I doing? Are you kidding me? You're alive, they're loving my meatballs, they're loving my *fish*! I'm out of chicken parmigiana, I'm out of lasagna—I'm out of my *head*. What a night! What a *night*!" He took Fonzie by the arm. Fonzie flinched in pain and pulled it back, but Al didn't notice. "I never would have made it," Al said. "I told myself I would have found a way. We accept things. You know? We get used to them. But now? Looking at it? It would have been horrible, Fonzie. Horrible. It would not have *worked*. Not for any of us. We need you on this earth. So please, stay on it, will you?"

There were kids there who must have been from the colleges. Marquette, or UW–Milwaukee. A group of them pushed through, getting between Al and Fonzie. Al had more food to run, so he waved at Fonzie and said he would see him around.

"Wow," one of the kids said, looking around, "this place is the real thing. Why haven't we ever come here before? What were we doing going to *Bennigan's* all this time?"

"From now on," another one said, "we party at Arnold's."

A chant rose up from the dance floor. Clapping and stomping. They were all looking at Fonzie. He waved them off.

Margo said to the Fonz, "What are they saying?" She listened. "Call sick? What's call sick?"

The Fonz said, "No, baby. Not call sick." He took a step forward. "They want the Cossack." Before she could ask what the Cossack was, he took off his jacket, handed it to her. He stepped onto the dance floor and was greeted by rapture. They cleared space for him. The band was drawing out the break, giving him a good groove to work with. He started off modestly, but as the pace of the music picked up, so did his flailing, his kicks and heel clicks. He gained momentum. Squatting down to the ground and springing up onto his heels, his arms and feet bursting forward and out. Then arms crossed, high-step kicking from a squat. The crowd clapped along, stomped their feet. They could not believe he still had it in him.

Twenty years ago he first executed the dance, right here on this very dance floor. It was a dance-a-thon. Richie's little sister, Joanie, was his partner. She wanted nothing in the world but to win, and Fonzie had promised to help her. He had been exhausted after fourteen hours of dancing. Then, like now, he was injured from a motorcycle accident. It seemed to be his fate to suffer for his passions then dance after. He seemed to be done. Could hardly stand up. He lost consciousness. The paramedics on-site were carrying him out on a stretcher. But Joanie knew what everyone knew, which is that the Fonz is never out. She stopped the stretcher and whispered into his ear: "If you don't get off that thing and keep dancing, I'm giving you a crew cut in your sleep." The threat to his hair was motivation enough. He was born again. He found the strength somewhere to climb off the stretcher and exhibit an impossible surge of crazed dancing to win it all. Somehow he danced harder, better, after he had seemed down for good. It was the same tonight—even his younger self would not have stood a chance against him now.

RICHIE WAS NOT ON THE DANCE FLOOR, HE WAS ON THE PAY phone near the bathrooms, shouting into the receiver, a finger jammed into his ear so he could hear. "Yeah, Mom, I know, you're right, I should've told you the truth. Now could you please put Lori Beth back on? Mom, listen, just focus on the good news, okay? He's *alive*. Fonzie's *alive*."

He hung up and rejoined the party. It was the best one Milwaukee had seen since the Brewers won the pennant. Richie hadn't been this ecstatic since Gleb Cooper called to tell him he had sold *Welcome to Henderson County*.

Gleb Cooper.

He had forgotten all about Gleb and his ultimatum. And here it was—Saturday night. The deadline. He had to call him. He had to give him his decision. What *was* his decision? What would he say? Would he really agree to write some awful thing that would completely annihilate whatever reputation he still had in the film industry, whatever little artistic integrity that remained after years of slow, steady compromise? Would he really degrade himself like that now? Did he really have to? He did, didn't he. Was this what it meant to grow up, to age? You became the person you told yourself you never would? Because you had to, just to survive?

It made his head hurt. It made his heart hurt.

He cooled off at the bar. A milk shake calmed him down, helped him think.

Fonzie appeared beside him, leaning against the bar. He was out of breath and, finally, perspiring, though trying not to let either one show. He glanced at Richie, saw his dour face. "Geez, Red," he said. "Who died?"

"You did," Richie said.

Fonzie nudged him with his elbow. "Can't get rid of me that easily."

"But I did, Fonz. For twenty years."

"Forget it."

"How can I? I'm sorry I lost touch."

"Nah, I'm the one who's sorry. When I heard about your dad, I just . . ." Fonzie looked away, down at the bar.

"I know," Richie said. He put his hand on Fonzie's shoulder. "I get it." Fonzie grimaced and put his hand on his lower back. "Still hurting pretty bad, huh, Fonzie?"

"I'm okay."

"Man, I can't believe it," Richie said. "You fell in love. In a way, Fonzie *is* dead. And Sealock did kill him—*Margo* Sealock."

"Now there's where you're wrong. Love never killed anybody."

Richie's smile disappeared.

"C'mon, Red. What's really eating at you?"

Richie told him—Gleb and *Space Battles* and *Suttree*. As Richie talked, it occurred to him: when he read *Suttree* he had a clear vision of the character, of the images he would put up on-screen. When he envisioned Suttree in his rowboat, on the river, resisting every current, his back was straight, his hands were up and out, gripping the oars, his face was squinted against the wind—it could have been something else he was riding along in. Not a boat at all—a 1949 Triumph with a silver gas tank, ape-hanger handlebars, front fender removed. He had been missing his friend so deeply, and he had not even realized it until he had found him in a book.

Fonzie said, "What do you want to do?"

"I don't know. I'll probably just take the job. It's the responsible thing to do."

"That's not what I asked you." Fonzie turned to him. "I asked you what you *want* to do."

"I want to tell him no. I want to make *Suttree*."

"Then that's what you gotta do."

"It's impossible, Fonz. I need five million dollars."

"Fine," said a voice behind them.

Margo.

"I'll be your producer," she said.

"If only you were serious," Richie said.

"I am completely serious. Our new Shotz Light has been a big success, business has never been better—I have the money."

"But then why did Martin need Sackett-Wilhelm? Why didn't he just get it from you?"

"I would have given it to him if he had asked. He knew that. But still he never asked. I think it was because he thought he had to do it all on his own. That was his curse, thinking that. But it doesn't really matter what he thought, or why he was the way he was. What matters is I have the money and I had it the whole time, and after all that's happened I don't want to stay in Milwaukee anymore. I don't want Martin Jr. growing up in a place where his name reminds everyone he meets of disgrace." She looked at Fonzie. "What do you think, Arthur?"

"It's riding season year-round out there, Fonz," Richie said. "And they can always use good stuntmen."

"Forget it," Margo said. "His days of flying off bridges are over." Fonzie bared his teeth, put his hand on his back again. "Know how he hurt his back?"

"Sure," Richie said, "the crash."

"Guess again."

"The Cossack?"

"*Opening a window.*"

Fonzie said, "Can you believe it? Nowadays, opening a window beats me up just as bad as crashing my bike."

"There's no hit man like time," Richie said.

"Hey, look," Fonzie said, "if moving to Hollywood means seeing my girl in a bikini on a regular basis *and* being near my old buddy? Count me in."

Men Who Work was finishing a tune by The Cars. The crowd applauded. "Thank you, thank you," Potsie said into the microphone. "And now for an original: it's a seventeen-minute multimovement rock opera about the history of Milwaukee manufacturing."

The crowd began dispersing for the bathrooms, the bar. Some booed.

"Where are you going?" Ralph said. "You're gonna love it, I swear, just wait until we get to the rap part." The few who had remained on the dance floor now joined the exodus.

Fonzie pushed himself off the bar. "I'll take care of this." He left Richie and Margo and limped over to the jukebox. He hit it with his elbow, and Bill Haley's voice filled the room.

"Rock Around the Clock."

The people cheered and stormed the dance floor all over again.

RICHIE PUT IN THE MONEY, DIALED GLEB COOPER'S OFFICE.

"Richard, how are you? You got news for me? I have a great big bottle of champagne in my hands. I'm ready for good news. I'm working the cork out, Richard. The cork is close, it's close.

Tell me you got good news so I don't waste all this brut. It's good brut, Richard, it's great brut."

"I'm sorry, Gleb. I'm sorry, but the answer is no. I just can't do it."

Gleb was silent for several seconds. "Part of me was hoping you'd say that. It's good to know there are still people out there who stand for something." Then he said, quiet and serious, "But you know what that means for us, Richard."

"I do."

"I wish it hadn't come to this."

"So do I."

"It's not personal."

"No. It's not. It's just the way it has to be."

"We did great work together."

Richie said, "Maybe one day the world will take another look at *Welcome to Henderson County.*"

Gleb scoffed. "No, that will never happen, Richard, that movie's dust. I'm talking about *Sorority Slaughterhouse.* You know about cable, don't you? Soon, Richard, as many as twenty-five percent of homes will watch cable TV. I just read it. Can you imagine? And this new cable channel, Cinemax? *Sorority Slaughterhouse* will *kill* on Cinemax, Richard. *Kill.* Your work will live on."

When Richie hung up, Fonzie was standing there. He had been listening. He put his arm around Richie, gave it a squeeze.

"Look out, California," he said. "Here we come."

• • • •

A CHEER ERUPTED THROUGH THE CROWD. TJ WAS WHEELING IN Fonzie's Triumph, completely restored to its original condition. Fonzie let out a low whistle and made his way over to it. He circled it, examining the work. His face was stoical, but when he spoke, his voice caught. "It's beautiful," he said. "I couldn't have done a better job myself."

It was the highest compliment.

He threw his leg over the bike—gingerly—and got on, turned the engine. It was loud. The cheering was louder. He revved it. It was better than any music.

Fonzie looked at Margo. He jerked his head at her to climb on. She came forward but remained off the bike. He cut off the engine. "What's the matter?"

She jerked her head toward the back of the bike and said, "Move it or lose it, gorgeous."

The crowd teased Fonzie, but he was scooting back, letting her get behind the handlebars. She kick-started the engine and revved it. The people cheered and cleared a path to the door. Fonzie held on tight to Margo. He winked goodbye to Richie, who waved back. "See ya later, Fonzie," he said. But the engine drowned him out. It didn't matter. There were no goodbyes.

They all followed the two of them outside. It was dark. The revolving *A* cast its neon glow on the pavement. Lieutenant Kirk stopped all traffic and waved Margo and Fonzie out into the road, both men giving small salutes to each other as they passed.

Margo opened it up, and it was not long before she and Fonzie disappeared into the night. Richie stood there in the parking lot among all those people—his people. His home. No matter where he was.

Then he went back inside. His friends were calling him to the stage. They had a guitar for him. The song was "Splish Splash." He hadn't played it since he was a kid. But he knew it would come back to him. It did not matter how long it had been. It was all there, everything he needed. It had been waiting for him all this time.

ABOUT THE AUTHOR

JAMES BOICE is the author of four previous novels: *The Shooting, The Good and the Ghastly, NoVA,* and *MVP.* He has contributed short fiction, journalism, and essays to such publications as *McSweeney's, Fiction, Salt Hill, Post Road, Salon, LitHub, The Daily Beast,* and *RollingStone.com.* Originally a native of California, he now lives and writes in Jersey City, New Jersey.